# The Company of Wolves
## (Learn to Howl book 3)
## Jennifer R. Donohue

For Jim

## Author Notes

Hello, and welcome to book 3 of the Learn to Howl trilogy. It has been quite the journey, in more ways than one! The trigger warnings that applied to the first two books are mostly present here, with a couple of additions. Thank you for trusting me on this journey.

It's *possible* (and I'm not making any promises with regards to, say, release dates), that you'll see another werewolf trilogy in the future. This one is from Morgan's perspective.

The werewolves in the Learn to Howl trilogy are different from typical movie werewolves; they are people and they are wolves, with no bipedal werewolf form in between. They're a little different from common pop culture urban fantasy werewolves; they're normal sized wolves, they don't communicate telepathically, and their social structures are more based on familial pack dynamics. I had a lot of fun with canine body language in the course of the trilogy, and maybe you will too!

Triggers warnings for The Company of Wolves include:

Medical experimentation

Kidnapping

Gunshot injury

Being drugged

Motor vehicle accident

Grief and grieving

# Chapter One

By the time we met up with the Wards, the sun was down and the night noises crackled out of the bushes on either side of the highway. They waited for us in a diner, and I went in as Morgan stopped outside to finish her cigarette. They looked up when I walked in, bells jangling overhead, or Luke and Joe did; Everett had his back to the door and was probably on his tablet or laptop. A pot of coffee was parked at the end of the table and menus were in front of our waiting places and I had a moment to think 'oh, my face' and then Joe's eyes got big, and he started to get up, but Luke put a hand on his shoulder. My face gave everything away, always. I knew it, they knew it, Morgan knew it.

I sat down with my back to the door, I'd make Morgan sit next to Luke. Everett moved his laptop over a little to give me space. "Morgan's outside," I said. "She'll be in." I realized I hadn't really spoken in hours.

"Allie?" Joe asked, frowning.

"I'm sorry, I can't," I said, tucking my chin and smiling down at my menu.

The waitress bustled over and I ordered me and Morgan bacon cheeseburgers, fries, milkshakes. I turned over my coffee mug, and Luke surprised me by reaching for the pot and pouring for me. The bells at the door jangled and I didn't need to look to know it was Morgan, and she strode across the room with that little hitch in her step and dropped into the booth across from me.

"Did you tell them?" she asked flatly, looking at me.

"No."

She smirked, like she expected as much, like she thought I was a coward. She looked around at the rest of the table. "Rachel said that if we didn't go back home after taking Allie's wolf to the sanctuary, then we shouldn't go home again." The waitress brought our milkshakes, vanilla, and Morgan flicked a smile at her and then sank a straw into hers.

"I'm really sorry," Joe said, looking at me.

"Yeah, them's the breaks, huh?" She sucked her cheeks flat on the milkshake, looked at me. I took a sip of my coffee. Nothing tasted like anything.

"Look, you don't—" Luke started. I couldn't begin to guess what Luke of all people was about to say to us.

"Shut the fuck up," Morgan said easily. "We made the choice we needed to make. You get anywhere on making a plan?"

A pause, as tense and fraught as any I'd ever taken part of, and I watched Luke's face, because I already knew what Morgan's had to offer. He was caught off guard, he was kind of pissed, and then he let it go. I didn't know why, but he let it go.

"Everett's been sorting through the clinic data," he said. "They left that USB in for a few days, I guess, and he's been all through the network."

Morgan turned her burning regard to Everett. The waitress slid our plates in front of us, looked at our faces and full water glasses, and walked away again without saying anything.

"The clinic is mostly just a normal fertility clinic, that I can tell," Everett said a little hesitantly, looking at Morgan, looking to Luke. "But sometimes they have more experimental patients, that they've done gene therapy on in utero. And patients with experimental medications after they're born, even if they weren't a fertility case to begin with? Or a couple, anyway."

"More of that Subject A type of business?" Morgan asked.

"Patient numbers, but yeah. Confidentiality." He paused, looked at his screen again. The worst thing that could happen right now, I thought, would be for him to say that he combed through the records and found that a batch of them matched the house that burned in Alabama. My house, except the Wards didn't know the whole of it. He looked around, looked at me. That was exactly what he'd found. God, did it even matter? Yeah, it mattered. Mama was why Silvernail knew about us. If Luke Ward knew that, and Bill, they wouldn't want to get her and the boys away from them anymore. Maybe the boys, maybe they'd just agree to save my brothers, if Everett said those things right now.

"Go on," Morgan said. She hadn't touched her food yet.

Everett dropped his eyes to his screen again. "But yeah, of course they want more of us to poke and prod. They had those couple days with the Culvers and then lost most of their research material. They want to use Annie and that lady and kids as bait, scoop up whoever comes for them."

"And that's just right there in the clinic data?" Morgan asked, sarcastically. She really had that tone where it felt like she was hitting you without moving a muscle. "They have a little powerpoint about kidnapping people for medical research?"

Everett shrugged a little. She wanted to fight somebody, he wasn't going to fight. Not only did people who fought with Morgan lose, but she also made them look bad. "That's not what their internal messaging says, but it's what their internal messaging says."

"So that's where we are? You didn't plan anything?"

"We didn't say that, Jesus." If we weren't sitting in a booth, Everett would've shoved his chair back from the table.

"Well quit fucking around then."

Luke looked like he was trying to coach himself into giving Morgan's behavior a pass. Quite the turnaround, and I couldn't figure out why he would be different. "The plan is, we're not going to agree to their meeting place, we—"

"We covered that, remember."

"Fucking eat your burger and listen," Luke snapped. Morgan's nostrils flared. We all waited for her to tear Luke's face off, except Luke, who kept talking instead. "We want to meet them in public, of course, and they had to expect that. Though keeping in mind what happened at the diner that you girls went to before, we need bigger, and more public." I flinched a little, without meaning to.

"The diner? Where police had to 'teargas protestors.'" Morgan made elaborate air quotes and then picked up her cheeseburger, so I guessed Luke played his cards right, somehow.

"Yeah, we haven't been able to track that PR spin just yet, if it came from the cops, or if they had newspaper sources to manipulate. But for location, we're thinking truck stop. There's too many civilians, too many variables. Of course, that means we'll have to play our own grab exactly right, but I think we've got a better chance than them."

"A truck stop? That's your plan?" I couldn't tell if she thought it was awful or awesome. I looked at Joe, who also did not seem to know. Who was also waiting for her to just explode, I thought.

"Yeah."

Morgan chewed for another minute. "Did they agree yet?"

Everett hit a button on the laptop. "Not yet."

"They will," I said, surprising myself a little. Surprising Morgan a lot, from her eyebrows. "To that, or something similar. Like you said, they had us for a little while. They're not going to be happy without us anymore." And they want to see how I've changed, I thought, looking down at my plate. They want to know where their control broke, and why I was able to change. Why their 'vitamins' stopped working. I was their long term project, maybe their first one. Maybe their only one, until they took the aunts. And I had no idea.

"I hate to bring this up, but should we lose Morgan's Jeep somewhere?" Joe asked, very hesitantly.

"Oh shit, yes we should," Morgan said. "Unless we want to use it as some kind of decoy at the truck stop? That sounds unhinged and appropriate."

"It kinda does," I said. "They'll know the Jeep. They probably wouldn't know whatever Luke's driving. Or we could steal something."

"What, you got the itch now?" Morgan asked, but less harshly. More like the normal kind of Morgan-teasing. She was so weirdly proud of me for that.

"Maybe I like showing off what you taught me," I said, because I was finally really starting to understand why she was just so much all the time. So angry, and abrasive, and aggressive. I was so tired, and so tired of crying.

"Is there anything else I can get you?" the waitress asked. "Do you want that boxed, hon?" She looked at my untouched plate.

"That's it, thanks," Luke said, leaning over to dig out his wallet, looking at the slip that she tore off and put in front of him.

"Thank you, yes," I said. I'd eat in the car, or wherever we were going next. It must be she had a dinner rush about to happen, and I didn't know how long Luke and Joe and Everett had held down this table already.

"Luke already reserved a couple rooms at the hotel by the highway," Joe said to me, and I was grateful for his sympathetic smile.

"Well good, we'll just move operation," Morgan said, standing up. "One of you want to come with and give us directions?"

"I will," Joe said.

"We'll see you there," Luke said. He stood up and got out his wallet, looked at two identical hotel keycards before handing one to Joe. "I guess that one's right."

"We'll figure it out." I half expected Morgan to snatch the card away, and I think Joe did too, but she didn't, just stood up and waited for me to get up, and then started walking. I waited for Joe before I followed her. I was tired of being alone with Morgan right now, even if Morgan was the one who also understood me best.

When we were far enough from Luke and Everett, but Morgan was still pretty much across the parking lot, Joe said, "I'm sorry about Rachel." I looked at him, startled. "When I was telling you about my dad, before, I didn't tell you that I was living with Grandpa because Dad didn't want me home anymore."

"Oh, God, I'm so sorry."

He shook his head, holding up a hand. "No, no, you don't need to do that. But I just wanted to tell you, so you'd know that I kind of understood. I know it's different but..."

"Thank you," I said. It isn't different, I wanted to say. Even if it wasn't the same either. Mama didn't want me because I'd become what she was afraid of. I wasn't what she wanted me to be. With Rachel...I thought she was still proud of us, even saw the sense in what we were doing, just couldn't join in. She had to protect her remaining sister, her pregnant niece, her doctor daughter. It just wasn't possible for her to do all of it. "Oh, we need to get moving, Morgan's going to—" on cue, Morgan tapped the horn, once.

"I expect nothing less," he said, smiling ruefully.

"I hope we made the right choice," I said as we started walking again. I didn't feel like it was something I could say to Morgan, without losing a tooth maybe. My untied bootlaces clattered against the pavement and Joe glanced down at them, then looked at me again.

"I think you did. And I think when all this is over, Rachel will let you come home again."

"I hope you're right." Wherever home would be then. In the pines again? Someplace else? She said they were going further to ground; was it a place that Morgan didn't know about either?

Joe climbed in the back of the Jeep and I got in the front and Morgan drove off without comment. The hotel wasn't far, a little concrete box with a flickering sign and rose bushes landscaping the parking lot, except deer had eaten them all down to sticks. Morgan grabbed both our bags, something I didn't expect, and she maybe hesitated a second, looking at the guitars in cases in the back, before slamming it all shut and nodding for Joe to lead us to the rooms.

Luke and Everett weren't far behind us. The rooms were across from each other on the end of the first floor, by the stairs and the ice machine and vending machines. The machines humming seemed very loud to me, but nobody else seemed to notice. Just new werewolf things I guessed. Still adjusting to what would've been a lifelong process. It hadn't even been a year yet, maybe I could've been more patient with myself if we weren't dealing with all this. None of this would've happened, if I'd been able to just grow up with my family like I was supposed to, Mama in the pines with her sisters, Morgan probably still bullying me because she was older, and she always had to be faster and better and just *more*. Morgan was the baby until I came along, I didn't think about that until just this second.

"Allie?" Joe asked. I was just kind of standing in the middle of me and Morgan's room, holding my boxed burger.

"Yeah, sorry." Apparently we were meeting across the hall, and I came over. The humming was a little more quiet there. "So where's the truck stop? Did they agree to it yet?"

"Ohio, and not yet. They'll probably email back in the morning."

"So, what—" Morgan started to ask, and then her phone rang and I about jumped out of my skin. I'd never heard her phone *ring*. She also looked slightly confused as she dug it out, then smiling, but still confused, she answered it. "Hunter, what's up?" She glanced up at us, then she went across the hall to our room, closing both doors behind her as she went.

"That happen often?" Luke asked, and I couldn't help but laugh.

"God, which part?" I asked.

"Hunter is Hunter Coutard?"

"Oh that? Yeah, she and Morgan are real close," I said, remembering what Morgan told me once about outing people. Or not outing people. "She doesn't normally call, though, she must've texted first." Morgan never ignored Hunter's texts, though. That I'd seen.

"Explains why she was with you miscreants at the diner," Luke said.

"Just the cost of inaction when Morgan is involved," Everett said.

"That so?" He was kicked back in a chair with his feet up on the corner of one of the beds. Then he nodded. "Sounds right."

"A legend of her time," I said dryly. I set the takeout box on the edge of the dresser and started to eat the burger, slowly, one handed, trying not to drop anything.

"You both have your strengths," Joe said.

"You don't have to be nice," I said. I actually wanted desperately for somebody to just be nice, and comforting, and also didn't know if I could handle it.

"I'm not." He looked around at us, flushed a little when he saw the intent look on Luke's face. "Morgan's got her style but you're more...thoughtful. So when the two of you, uh, present a case it ends up working out. And you can kind of smooth people out when they're all worked up."

"Yeah, it works real good with Morgan." I shook my head. But I was flattered, and maybe a little flustered, and I closed the takeout box and hoped that Luke wouldn't ruin this.

But Luke said, "Joey's kind of right, though. She bulldozes everything and you present a saner case. We never would've worked with just Morgan, but then you opened your mouth."

Now I was very flustered, because I'd never much thought about how Luke, or Bill, thought of me other than whether I was blending well enough as a wolf. Whether I was too hesitant, too soft, not enough like Morgan. Who actually saved me from having to make further comment by coming back then.

"Okay, Hunter'll be able to be an alternate vehicle for us, after we ditch the Jeep," she said.

"Oh that's good," I said, blinking. That was fast. "I'm surprised she's not grounded for a million years or whatever."

"Ardith isn't her mother," Morgan said. "And we're all adults." The corner of her mouth twitched just a little when she said it; I wasn't an adult, quite, and it wasn't that she had a tell when she was lying normally, it was that she thought it was so damn funny that the Wards didn't know about me. Normally, you couldn't tell at all when Morgan was lying.

"Just blows the mind, the Coutards involved," Luke said.

"Just Hunter and just as herself. Insomuch as we're all just individuals, and not some kind of big weird organization that you Wards seem to want. Wouldn't that be something, though, if we could get all the families in on it? Safety in obscurity stopped working, time for strength in numbers."

"Could that ever happen though?" I asked.

Morgan and Luke looked at each other and shrugged. Everett looked up from his screen. "Yeah, maybe. It'd have to come from the Coutards, though, since they're pretty much the ones who know everybody. All of us know some families, maybe Rachel a little more since she's helped with peacekeeping some."

There was a pause, and then Luke said, "Well if we're just sitting around waiting for them to email us back, we might as well get some shuteye. You kids want to keep talking, you can do it in the other room."

"Kids, right," Morgan grinned. "Because you're so ancient. You probably don't want to make this weird."

"Morgan," I said. She ignored me, still looking at Luke.

"I'm twenty seven. You never asked."

"Maybe I should've, that's a special number amongst my people."

"It is?" I didn't know anything about twenty seven, from any of the Culver stuff I'd read or been told, and she gave her mean laugh.

"Rock stars. Twenty seven is significant amongst rock stars." I blinked at her. "I swear to Christ, Allie, the things you don't know sometimes."

"Sorry, right, I wasn't thinking about how you're a rock star at every waking moment, sorry. I don't know how I can forget, the way we listen to *your* music at all times. I'm surprised you don't have a tattoo of your own name." God I was so tired and didn't know why I said any of that. So much for smoothing people over being one of my strengths. Or my only strength.

Incredibly, though, or because she was Morgan, she laughed. "We should do that, get tattoos when all this is over. I know a great place in Point Pleasant."

"Morgan, what would I even get a tattoo of."

"Well if you don't have something in mind ahead of time, there's always flash to pick from on the wall." She picked up my leftovers and popped open the lid to steal some french fries. "You got any tattoos, Luke?"

"Yeah, I'll show you, but everybody else has to leave," he said, matching her grin.

"Scandalous," she said. "Okay, let's get outta here and I'll put Cinderella to bed before she turns into a pumpkin."

"That isn't the story," I said, but she was herding me out the door and I had no interest in protesting.

"Yeah, I know, but sometimes it's more interesting to change things around. Everett, you fucking tell me the second you get an answer in the email or I swear to god I'll make guitar strings out of your guts. I read up on how to do it when I was out of commission last winter."

"Jesus, yes, I'll tell you."

"Goodnight boys." She shut their door on their answer and we went across the hall. "God they're exhausting."

"*They're* exhausting," I repeated, mystified. She closed our door and kicked her boots off before throwing herself across a bed and turning the TV on.

"Well I'm exhausted anyway. You want the rest of this?"

"No, you can finish it." I kicked my boots off, more slowly. Morgan's phone buzzed, and she put it on the bed in front of her so she could poke at the buttons. "Tell Hunter I say hi."

"Will do," she said, not looking up.

# Chapter Two

I slept through the night but I felt like I kept waking up, gasping like something in my dream was going to get me, but I didn't remember what any of it was. The blue light of Morgan's TV would be there, though, and it hurt to roll over to see if she was awake so I didn't do that, just always closed my eyes and tried to drift off again.

A knock at our room door really woke me up though, and Morgan had it open and was talking to Everett before I even finished sitting up.

"They agreed to the truck stop," he said.

"Well that's both good and bad, isn't it."

"Sure is." He looked past her at me. "Morning, Allie."

"Hey, Everett."

"Alright so we'll get hosed off and then come over and talk general strategy. How we'll use the Jeep as bait/distraction."

"Sounds good."

Morgan turned up the TV after she shut the door, just the weather channel. "You gonna be okay, seeing your mama and brothers?"

"I guess," I said. "More okay than thinking they're getting experimented on. Though I guess Mama signed up for that, didn't she? But the boys deserve better."

"It's not like we can keep 'em, Allie," she said.

"They're not like the wolf, I know. It wasn't like I could keep him either."

"You tried," she said, surprising me. I looked at her, struggling with the impulse to hug her for suddenly being a kind and caring cousin, and with the idea that she was playing some kind of long joke on me and I shouldn't trust her at all. I could trust Morgan with my life, that was for damn sure, but not with my feelings.

"I did. It's all we can ever do, I guess."

"Got that right." She rummaged in her bag. "I'm gonna shower quick, unless you want to go first and have the recovery time?"

"Oh, I guess I should." I should have asked her to help me but I wasn't going to ask her to help me. Probably, if I'd actually stayed put and gotten bed rest, my collarbone would feel a lot better by now. The silver bullet wound, probably not. Even Morgan's non silver bullet took months, and she still didn't walk exactly right. Maybe she never would again.

When I was done, I sat on the bed and waited for Morgan, and she braided her hair and then mine without me having to ask. Then she stomped into her boots and went across the hall and I got my feet into my boots and looked unhappily at the laces before following.

"Okay, so truck stop?" she said as soon as I was there.

"Truck stop," Luke said. "We figure you two go in with the jeep, like you intend to leave with the woman and boys in the Jeep. They won't know my pickup, it'll be a crunch but we can fit everybody in the short term, then once we're clear, we meet Hunter with whatever your alternate vehicle is."

Morgan considered a minute. "Sounds simple, sounds good. About what I was thinking."

"So you're not going to argue?"

"No, why would I argue? It's a fine plan."

"So we're relying on the notion there's going to be a crowd at this place and that's it, to keep us away from the mad scientists?" Joe asked.

"Yeah. You'd think we'd all be smarter than that, right?" Morgan laughed. "They don't want anybody to know. If there's enough people, inside and out, truckers and families and what have you, that's too much for Silvernail to deal with. More than seven people in a sleepy diner in the evening. Twenty four hour truck stops are what they are."

"If you say so." Joe's tone was at his most dubious.

"Don't tell me you've never been to a place like this."

"Alright, I won't tell you," Joe said affably.

"Oh buddy, you are in for a treat. Well. Other than the Silvernail worries. But you-all will be an unknown factor for them."

"We were with you in—" Everett started.

"Oh I know but they didn't get footage of that, not really. So we're good."

Luke squinted a little. "You know this makes me think that you're not going to stick to the plan."

"I'll stick to the plan! Jesus, what do I need to do, pinkie swear?" She was smiling, really delighted. Also really telling the truth, I thought. Had she lied to me yet? Had I caught her lying to me yet? I looked at Joe, who shrugged a little.

"No, I don't want you to pinkie swear." Luke considered a minute. "Allie, will you try your damndest to get her to stick to the plan, such as it is?"

I gave a surprised laugh. "I appreciate that you think I can affect her behavior, but yeah. We all want this to happen."

"There, see, Allie's my conscience, it'll work out." She grinned at them, and at me.

"Well okay then. We'll drive on up to Ohio and get this done."

"And then after?" I asked, before I could stop myself, and everybody looked at me. "What comes after. How are we going to make them stop?"

"I don't have the answer to that," Luke said. "Bill says he's working on it, and when we're in the field like this, it's better if we don't have enough information that can be harmful. In case we get picked up."

"Makes sense," Morgan said. "Also, what do you have for armory?"

Luke blinked, but I didn't know how she could catch him off guard with a question like that, given what we were doing. "You can throw an eye on the gun rack, if you want. Otherwise, I'm the only one licensed to concealed carry in the states we're going through. Unless there's something you're not telling me."

"I mean, I'm sure there is, but that isn't it. Good to know."

"Well what do *you* have?"

"Same rifle that Allie used back when, and a shotgun. And old trusty, that's what I just decided to call the baseball bat. That name changes. The tire iron's just a tire iron."

"We aren't going to need any of that at a crowded truck stop," I said, more wishing than making a declaration.

"No, probably not," Luke said.

"No, but maybe after." Morgan shrugged. "And maybe not."

"Alright, let's hit the road. We'll coordinate when we need to make a stop, sound good?"

"Oh yeah, roger that," Morgan said, smirking.

Joe stopped me on the way out of the room. "Hold on," he said. I looked at him, then watched Morgan cross the hall for our stuff.

"What?"

"Let me get these for you." And he dropped to one knee and tied my boots for me.

"You don't have to—" But he was done by the time I tried to say anything. I was trying to ignore Luke in the hallway; Everett was out at the truck already.

"I could tell how unhappy it was making you," he said as he got up, and this time, I was the one who blushed.

"Thank you."

"You're welcome. I hope—"

"Allie let's gooooooo," Morgan foghorned from down the hallway.

"I need to..." I said.

"I know, it's okay."

Luke wasn't right outside the door the way I thought he was, he was by the exit, maybe watching Morgan go to the Jeep. "Drive safe," he said, like I'd be the one driving.

"That is out of my hands," I said, and he laughed. He said something to Joe that I didn't catch as the door closed behind me.

"What were you doing?" Morgan asked, when I got myself in the jeep.

"Joe tied my boots for me."

She looked mystified. "Did you want your boots tied? You didn't ask me to."

"No, I didn't ask you to. You're already doing so much, I don't want to be even more of a pain." I already ruined your life, I don't want you to have to tie my boots too, I couldn't say. She looked at me, but she was wearing sunglasses and I could only imagine the glare, or the assessment. She did that on purpose, wearing sunglasses as much as she did, there was no way it wasn't part of her dominance and intimidation game. She even wore them on her album covers. I assumed she wore them on stage too, and maybe that was part of how she handled the lights and everything.

"I don't know what you need unless you tell me," she said, following Luke's truck out of the parking lot.

"I know." What a weird conversation this was to be having with her. "I try not to need too much. I've needed so much."

She laughed. "Allie you got *shot*."

"So did you."

"And I was an absolute fucking gem in the first months of my recovery, and continue to be a model patient." She laughed. "It's not like I don't *know*."

"Then why—"

"Not knowing and not stopping myself are two different things." She poked the cassette sticking out of the tape deck until it fed in and Howling started.

"Did you, uh..." It really would've helped if we always called it the same thing. Morgan waited me out, though. "When you were still really laid up, did you ever change. To see if it would help?"

"I did, and it didn't." She was frowning and this time I waited. "I don't know if it would help you. Like...wolves don't have collarbones, right?"

"I don't—"

"Wait, no wolves do, but dogs don't. Isn't that wild?"

"I guess? Yes?" I never thought very much about collarbones in general, or mine specifically, until one was broken.

"So yeah, changing would probably suck a fuckton. And make it suck even more when you change back. Not that I thought you were all about experimenting."

"Yeah no, I'm not."

"Prob'ly safer that way. Christ, does it have to be so sunny?"

"I think that happens a lot in the summer. I could be wrong."

She laughed, lighting a cigarette. "Oh now who's the smartass?"

I wanted to talk about Rachel, or Mama, or the plan, but couldn't bring myself to do it. I just didn't know what to say, and didn't want to upset the balance of whatever sort of not-bad mood Morgan was in. I hesitated to call it good, or even cheerful. Maybe it was because she was going to get to see Hunter. I wasn't even sure if I should talk about the Wards too much, so I just tried to sleep more instead.

Morgan shook me awake around noon, and I blearily followed her into the convenience store. She threw away a paper cup as we went, which meant she stopped for coffee at least once without waking me, but I couldn't really say I minded. I was hit by the realization that I was going to see Mama again, *today*, and even though I'd known that, I hadn't really processed it. I stopped, stricken, in front of a sunglasses display. I expected Morgan to clomp on, oblivious, but she turned immediately.

"Aviators," she said.

"What?" I blinked at her. The fluorescents were very loud overhead.

"Aviators are what looks best on us, I think. Go for aviators."

"I wasn't looking for—"

"Joe, come here!" she called, and Joe's head popped up over by the soda cooler. "We need your opinion."

"Okay." He seemed confused, but made his way over. There were a few other people here, but it wasn't crowded. Luke was waiting for the new pot of coffee to brew, and Everett examined a display with plugs and wires. Device charging stuff.

"I think Allie should get aviators," Morgan said, spinning the rack and finding a silver-rimmed pair. "What do you think?" She shoved them on my face and started to turn me, stopped when I flinched away and turned myself.

"I think they look good," he said. Firmly, like he was keeping himself from wavering, or saying too little or too much.

I looked at the little peeling mirror on the spinning rack. "Well thanks." I guessed they looked okay. I didn't know what others I'd pick for myself, honestly. It was the style Morgan always wore, and I both did and didn't want to be just like her. "I guess we better not waste too much time, though. I'm going to go to the bathroom, if you wouldn't mind getting me one of those slushie things?"

"I'm so glad you've embraced the junk food lifestyle, cuz, I was starting to think you were one of those weirdo Christians who didn't celebrate Halloween."

"Well. I was." And for once I was able to get away having fired the parting shot, even as I realized I shouldn't have said anything like that in front of Joe. I trusted Morgan could handle any questions, if he asked any questions, and by 'handle the questions' I meant railroading him in a different direction the way she did to everybody. Like she'd just done to me.

When I got out of the bathroom and looked around, everybody else had gone back out to the vehicles. Joe waited for me with a slushie drink and a pair of sunglasses. "Morgan said you absolutely had to have them," he said with a shrug. "She brought the food to the car."

"I'm glad she doesn't make sense to anybody else either, or I'd question my sanity."

"She must make sense to herself."

"I suppose that's true."

In the parking lot, Morgan and Luke were loading the stuff from the back of the Jeep into the back of his pickup, which both had an extended cab and a cap on the bed. "I don't see how a person needs three guitars," he was saying when Joe and I walked up.

"Oh, one of the acoustics is Allie's," she said.

"Alright." Luke looked at me, shrugged, and picked up an amp.

"No, I gotta know, is that more reasonable, one acoustic and one electric for me?" She grinned. "Of course, that's one acoustic and one electric in standard tuning. Normally, I like to keep one around that's in drop D. That's the sound of grunge, of course, and works good for my kind of metal. Sometimes I've got a baritone too, they're really good for chugging, which we don't do a whole lot, but it's an effective motif. Fender also came out with these real weird acoustic electrics that the switch like, tries to make it sound like the guitar you're holding is physically different? I only messed around with one once at a guitar show, they look weird too, not my style at all but you don't wanna dismiss things out of hand, y'know?"

"Who knew you were an equipment nerd," Everett said from the open passenger window.

Morgan laughed. "We've all got our niche, right? I didn't even get into pedals at all. Careful of this by the way, it's my pedalboard. I'll bet Luke here could go on for awhile about the merits of the M16 or something. Whatever SEALs are using nowadays. Is it actually the M16?"

He cleared his throat. "It's the FN SCAR actually."

"Yeah see. And you could talk to me about loadouts and what other kinds of weapons take the same UN rounds and all kinds of things, couldn't you?"

"If I tell you that I see your point, will you quit it?" I laughed, and he sighed.

"Yeah maybe." Morgan tossed our bags in the back of the truck, surveyed the jeep. "Oh fuck, my tapes." She crawled fully into the back of the jeep, then climbed over into the back seat, coming up with a reusable shopping bag that she started gathering cassettes into.

"Do you want help?" Joe asked.

"Sure, thanks," she said, muffled but vigorous, and Joe found a tote bag and started gathering tapes from the front.

"Are these all yours? I mean, all Howling?"

She hopped out with her full bag. "A lot of 'em, but no. Some are other projects, and some are friends. Well and some are concerts we played so yes again."

"Cassettes," Luke said and Morgan pushed past him too hard on purpose.

"Of course. Nothing beats the sound of a cassette." They stowed the tapes in the back and Morgan surveyed the jeep with her hands on her hips. "I guess that's as good as it's gonna get. Let's get rolling."

"I guess good luck, if we don't stop again in between."

"You could almost be accused of having a heart, Luke." She patted his cheek and we got back in the jeep.

# Chapter Three

There was a real big chicken statue, out front of the truck stop, and Morgan slowed down and took a picture of it with her phone like she was just a terrible tourist. I kept my eyes peeled for Annie, or Mama and the boys, or people I thought were Silvernail ready to tranquilize us and drag us off to labs. I didn't see any of those things, not right away.

Morgan looked at me. I'd taken off my sling again, and I couldn't decide if it was the worst idea or if it was going to be alright. It was probably nearing the time I could've taken the sling off in general, if I'd actually followed medical advice. Morgan clearly didn't know which either because I would've heard either verdict by now if she decided. "I'm gonna ask you one last time if you think you can handle this."

I took a breath. I appreciated her asking, but it was kind of too late. "I have to. We don't have any other way to do it."

"I guess it is a little late for second guesses." She shrugged. "What are your brother's names, anyway?"

"Kevin and Jason." It seemed like I could hardly remember their faces. They were years younger than me, enough that playing with them was more something I did because I was supposed to be watching them, not because we wanted to be doing the same things. They were pains in the ass. They might think I was some kind of a demon now, depending on what Mama said to them, and Daddy. Had they been praying I wouldn't come back and hurt them? Had they just been forbidden to talk about me? My presence from the house erased. One of them moved into my bedroom. Oh Jesus, maybe this was a bad idea. We were putting everybody here at risk.

"Kevin and Jason. Okay. Keep your sunglasses on."

"What?"

"It's bright out." Morgan held the door for me and we walked into the big restaurant food court area, corridor to bathrooms leading off to the right. I smelled Mama first, the hand lotion she always used, and I think that's when my heart hardened against her finally. Silvernail people shot Daddy dead and buried him in the woods like a dog, but Mama found the time to pack the hand lotion she liked best. Then I saw the boys, each with a comic book, not something they'd ever been allowed to have at home. They seemed okay and smelled okay and I was relieved, so relieved, but I didn't feel the surge of love I thought I might and that made me feel guilty. Like maybe I was a little bit the monster that Mama seemed to think I was, not loving my brothers. Hating my mama.

Annie was there too of course, fidget-nervous and on her feet soon as Morgan and I walked in, eyes darting this way and that, so I'd guess Morgan at least had an idea of who the Silvernail folks in the room were. I gave an experimental sniff anyway, and was caught up a little short. I thought I recognized one of them, from that night they burned Mama and Daddy's house. I looked around too, but it didn't help.

Mama stared at me, her mouth open a little. We kept our sunglasses on, and the whole room felt electrified, and like I was aware of every last person in it, there were so many people, all moving around and standing in line and sitting down and getting up, shuffling past to the bathroom, brushing past on phone calls and laughing together and lighting cigarettes the second they were outside. I could smell gun oil and silver and something else, maybe tranquilizers. Yes, tranquilizers, I'd never smelled them before without also choking on smoke. "Alleluia," Mama said, getting to her feet. The boys looked up and then ran at me full force, both of them wrapping their arms around my waist after we collided, and I reflexively hugged them back while hissing air through my teeth because my collarbone and shoulder weren't thanking me at all for any of this. Morgan glanced at me, and I could practically see her thoughts, that I was all tangled up with the boys and was already slowed down besides. Then she was grinning white teethed and hard at Annie and Mama. "Glad we're all punctual."

Annie stared at Morgan and then at me, and the math she was doing was plain on her face. Morgan and I weren't close enough looking to be mistaken as twins, but we looked more like sisters than cousins even to the Wards. I guessed maybe some more pieces were falling into place for poor Annie, especially as Mama had a family resemblance still, except everything was a little less vivid with her. Brown hair not black, brown eyes, not ice blue. And then the boys, another step. Plus, Annie would know if the boys had at one point had a girl twin each. This was the worst time to be thinking about that, I had to focus.

Annie was anxious too and I wasn't any kind of psychic and the boys were squeezing me and I was starting to sweat, panting a little, and I was trying to mark the people in the room I thought were our enemies, which was a harder thing to do than you'd think. One of these people could be the person who shot me with silver, knowing full well what it'd do to me. There was a certain coldness in a person's heart to do that, there had to be.

Shooting with silver and burning people's houses. Morgan had to know already, I had to assume Morgan knew already, she was better than me at everything.

Mama had come almost to me, but stopped more than an arm's length away. Annie was smiling desperately, but I didn't hear what she was saying to Morgan. I looked at Mama and she tried to look at me, and sunglasses weren't the problem. She was afraid, and I didn't know if she was afraid of me or afraid of what was going to happen. She was more than afraid and I couldn't sort it all out right now. "Alleluia," she said, her voice quieter, but I didn't hear any love in it. She didn't want me to hurt the boys, maybe that was it. Didn't want the boys hurt and didn't see how she could yank them away from me without causing a big scene here in public.

"Hi, Mama."

"I told you my sisters would take care of you," she said, pleading.

"You did, and they have. Better than you ever did." That hurt her, but not enough. It was childish to want to hurt her, but I couldn't let it go. She used to hit me. She thought I was a monster. Daddy was dead. Daddy was dead and she had her damn hand lotion. "Dulcie died," I said, and she flinched, catching her bottom lip between her teeth.

"I thought—" she said, and then stopped herself.

"Who's Dulcie?" Kevin asked, looking up at me. "Mama has sisters?"

"Yeah, kiddo, she has sisters." Two left, I didn't say.

"Can we meet them?" Jason asked, twisting around to look back at Mama.

"Maybe," she said in that voice that I knew meant absolutely not. "Why don't you two let go of Allie? She probably can't hardly breathe."

"You said she was in Africa but she doesn't look like it," Kevin said.

"Maybe she finally listened to me about sunscreen," Mama said, too brightly, holding out her hand to them. "Come on now." Slowly, they unwound their arms from me and backed up, but Kevin caught my left hand in his, and drew me a couple steps closer to Mama. I looked around the truck stop; more people here than there were in that diner, Morgan was right of course. I looked at her, and she looked at me and raised her eyebrows, tilted her head a little. I followed the dotted line, and there was a county sheriff laughing and talking with one of the waitresses, holding his Styrofoam cup of coffee. We *thought* that would mean Silvernail wouldn't go guns blazing. Fingers crossed, and maybe a little prayer.

I touched my cross, probably something I did a lot without realizing, but I heard Mama's little intake of breath. "But that's silver," she said, so very quietly, looking at me differently again. With regret, like she'd made the bad decision, and I almost let her keep on thinking that she'd made that mistake, that silver didn't hurt me any more now than it had the day I was born. But I couldn't go on needing Mama. Not after what she'd done, and been willing to do. I had Morgan, and maybe I'd have Rachel and Sela again. Sidney. Fran.

I kept my voice quiet too, my tone clipped. "Rachel got me a copy." I didn't know what Morgan and Annie were saying to each other but it seemed to me like Annie was actually still on our side. Morgan would be more angry if she wasn't. For all the good that did us in the long run but right now we needed to use that to make our escape. Morgan would find a way to make it work, I was sure of it, and then I felt just a little bit better, because we all had our moments of doubt and maybe I'd just gotten through another one of mine.

Mama's face fell again just like that, the hopefulness draining away, and I still had Kevin's hand and reached out for Jason's as she started to recoil, my shoulder hollering at me but not screaming yet. I hoped they'd just come, I couldn't pick one of them up like this. They were too big anyway. Morgan finished up with Annie, pulled out her phone for a second and texted something, nodded and dropped it in her back pocket again. Then she came over to the little group of Mama and the boys and me, startled Mama about out of her skin by giving her a big strong hug. "Aren't reunions nice?" she asked, grinning still, in that way that wasn't really joy but a threat. Though Morgan certainly took joy in making threats.

"They are," Mama said uncertainly, looking from Morgan to Annie, who was now doing something on her phone, moving closer to the sheriff.

"Let me help you with the bags, Aunt Joyce," Morgan said, guiding Mama, who moved away when either of us came closer to her. Who was trying to look for Annie, trying to look around the room. Maybe she knew who the Silvernail people were, who were supposed to somehow grab up the rest of us, like we were stray dogs coming to food put out in a trap.

"Well okay," Mama said, fully flustered now, which I knew because I'd known her so well or thought I'd known her so well, even if I couldn't smell her nerves, her fear. The boys were just excited, not scared, and smelled like sweat and sunlight and fried food. I wondered if McDonald's had been the revelation for them that it had been for me. Probably not; they were younger and hadn't thought about it as much.

Morgan and Mama took those couple steps to grab the two overnight bags that were stowed under the table, and were on their way back to me and the boys when Annie made an indescribable noise and dropped her phone, right next to the sheriff. He was an older man, and he didn't startle like maybe she was hoping, but he perked right up, turning to her. He gave the rest of the room a quick scan, not seeming to stop on the little group of us moving to the door, all the adults at a glance looking pretty similar to one another, but he did pause on somebody to the right of us, and I turned too, in time to see one of the people who smelled like gun oil and something else putting their hands flat on the table, next to their untouched silverware. Their pancakes looked pretty cold by now.

I followed that person's gaze to a blonde woman at another table, who stirred her coffee with an unnecessary force. That was two, there had to be more, I thought. Neither of them were the one that smelled familiar. But knowing two of them was better than knowing none of them. And they were trying to watch both us and the sheriff. I could see the jeep from the window, they had to as well. They were getting up by the time we cleared the door.

And then we were back out in the sunlight again, Mama and the boys blinking and shielding their eyes against the sun as Morgan hustled them across the sundrenched parking lot in the opposite direction from the jeep, chattering the whole while about how they were going to have a nice family vacation and meet the parts of the family they hadn't met before, but it's where Allie lived now and she was having a real good time except for missing everybody else. She was a stunning liar, just stunning, and I tried not to look behind us too many times, tried not to look at the jeep at all, as I waited for the boys and Mama to get into Luke's truck, as I got myself into Luke's truck and then Morgan crammed in too.

"Everybody buckled who can be?" Luke asked, but he was already driving away at a leisurely pace, in the line of cars to leave the parking lot but without his turn signal on.

"Yessir," Kevin said, and Jason echoed him a second later, half in Mama's lap, fastening the buckle around them both. Maybe he'd hoped to get away without it, a possibility that had maybe never entered the vistas of his imagination before this adventure he was on.

"Good, thank you." Luke glanced at Mama in the rearview mirror, and then me and Morgan, but I couldn't read his expression. I couldn't tell what mental math he was doing. Morgan was texting and after a second looked up.

"Okay, Hunter's going to meet us across the Pennsylvania state line, at another one of those deer antler motels, she says."

"Deer antler motels?" Luke asked.

"Yeah, you know the type. Here, Everett, put this in the GPS." She leaned forward with her phone.

"Does Hunter have your jeep replacement already?" I asked. I didn't think about *where* we were taking Mama and the boys right now, the Wards I assumed. Hunter is probably better.

"Well, no. But there's only so much longer you're gonna last today, so we'll spend the night. And then Hunter will take your—take Joyce and the boys to Ivy's granddaughter Betty in...oh well she's in Ohio isn't she. Hmm." She frowned, sent another message.

"Oh, I'm sure she's delighted with that. And...Joyce will be too." Mama wasn't saying anything, just sitting very upright against the car door, her hands folded in her lap. I wondered if she'd try to run when we stopped, and that was a strange thought to have. Mama running.

"I think it probably beats the alternative," Morgan muttered. "Anyway, how you holding up?"

I started to just say fine, I'm okay, automatically and I stopped myself and actually took a few breaths. "Kind of wishing Dr. Fran's prescription hadn't run out," I admitted.

"Oh, I held a few back actually."

"Morgan."

"Don't be like that, pills aren't my thing. It just didn't make sense to wake you up to take them if you were sleeping okay, and you sleep way sounder than I do. Like a rock." Despite the close quarters, she twisted around in the seat, sliding the rear window open and fishing her arm back through until whatever she touched rattled, and pulled the bag up high enough to get the pill bottle out of.

"I always have," I said. "Though that makes me worry about what you might do when I'm sleeping."

I expected her to laugh, but she kind of sharpened up a little. "Does it?"

"Yeah I'll have to check the mirror for drawn on mustaches or something."

"Well now that you gave me the idea..." She laughed then. We were all so keyed up. "And anyway, I can still try to call Fran once you really run out."

"Can you?"

She blinked, as if never being able to call her sister again, even though she never called her sister in the first place, hadn't occurred as an option. "Well I assume."

"We can get you to Tyler's again if you need that looked at," Luke said over his shoulder. I hadn't been thinking about the other people in the car, but the boys were already bored with us and quietly bickering about something, and Mama was staring across the tops of their heads at me and Morgan.

"We don't need to go all the hell back down to Georgia," Morgan said. "No matter how good a field surgeon he is."

"Thanks though," I said. I wished I had a bottle of water, something, but managed to swallow the pill anyway, sharp-edged all the way down.

"Yeah, no problem," Luke said, like we were having the most casual conversation. "Getting shot sucks."

"Sure does," Morgan said.

"Alleluia, why are you...people talking about getting shot?" Mama asked suddenly. The way she stumbled over calling us people almost made me throw that pill back up again.

"Because I got shot." I felt a grim satisfaction in seeing her flinch. Was this what Morgan felt like, all the time? "With silver."

"Oh, Allie," she said with a sigh, and I couldn't tell if she was even more disappointed in me or scared for my hurt or what. She'd been so nice to me that final night, before she packed me in the car to the aunts. She hadn't wanted me to be hurt then either, had taken good care of me. She was my mother, of course she'd take good care of me. But she'd also abandoned me and thought I was a demon, and was clearly terrified and disgusted by my presence. Oh why was this so hard. "I've been praying for you."

I thought again of Daddy in the woods. I took a deep breath of the scent of her hand lotion. "I doubt it," I said. She would've hit me for that, back home, and I stared at her so she knew that we were both thinking about that. She sighed, and turned her head to look out the window.

# Chapter Four

Once we felt like we'd made our immediate getaway, Luke pulled over so that Everett and Morgan could get in the bed of the truck, and I sat up front with Joe and Luke. Joe saw the look on my face and took the middle seat without any pause. I reached over and turned on the radio; I wasn't used to driving in a quiet car anymore, and I couldn't face the horror of trying to make any kind of small talk with Joe *and* Luke *and* Mama *and* Morgan. I hit seek a couple of times, with it stopping on talk radio, and country, and finally hit what I thought seemed like a rock station.

"Oh fuck this is The Brians," Morgan said from the way-back. I looked over my shoulder, catching a glimpse of Mama's scandalized face starting to color, my brothers' eyes getting big. I wondered how many times they'd heard the f word. Enough to know it was bad, I guessed. "We're supposed to play a festival with them next year."

"The Brians?" I asked before anybody else could.

"Yeah these guys, it's hilarious but also they keep succeeding for no reason and I hate them. And not a single damn one of them is named Brian."

"What?" Was I egging her on to needle Mama? Maybe. "Why are they named The Brians if none of them are named Brian?"

"Legend says they wanted to be named The Brains because they were all honors students in high school, but they were laid low by a typo."

"Is that true?"

"Fuck if I know, the drummer not-Brian grabbed my ass at a show once and I broke his nose."

"Morgan!" I wasn't really shocked; I'd seen Morgan break somebody's nose before.

"He's lucky that's all I did."

Mama cleared her throat. "If we could keep the language clean. For the boys."

"Oh shit, sorry Joyce," Morgan said, and I saw the flash of her teeth, and Luke laughed.

Kevin, who had been craning his neck back and forth, said in a too-loud whisper "She looks like Allie."

"Yes, she does," Mama said in a clipped voice that said children should be seen and not heard. But, emboldened by Morgan's cursing, probably, he sat up straighter. Besides the fact that Mama never hit the boys.

"Why do you look like Allie?" he asked Morgan, and I saw her grinning again, like the big bad wolf.

"Because we're cousins," she said. I was *very* aware of all of the Wards in the car not saying anything, just listening to this play out.

"We don't have any cousins," Kevin said.

"Allie does," Mama said, even more icily.

"That doesn't make sense," Jason said, looking up from his comic book.

"But it's true," Mama said. "And you are not going to take that tone with me."

"I was just *saying*," Jason said with a whine creeping into his voice.

"Jason."

"Sorry, Mama."

"I'm sorry too, Mama," Kevin said, just to preempt her.

"It's okay just hush now, and you can watch television at the hotel." She looked at me, to give me her 'and I'll deal with you later young lady' look, but when our eyes met, her shoulders dropped, and she looked out the window again.

I turned back around, and The Brians finished their song. I didn't know the next band, but I guess Morgan didn't either, because she didn't say anything.

• • • •

"YOU PICK PLACES LIKE this on purpose," Morgan said, when we got to the antler motel and met up with Hunter.

"Caught me red-handed," she grinned. "I love them so much. Just look at it!" It was a lot like the place we'd stayed at in Tennessee actually. Lots of birch with the bark still on it, lots of antlers and mounted taxidermy, even on the outside. Gravel parking lot, red neon signs. "They even have a restaurant, so it's a step up from the usual. With a fireplace."

"Ooh a fireplace, just when it's coming in summer," Morgan said, teasing but not mean. She wasn't mean to Hunter, or they were both the same kind of mean and it canceled out. I watched Luke take it in, but I couldn't read his face.

"It's for the *atmosphere*, you barbarian."

"Right. Lemme tell you about the atmosphere of having a fireplace your entire life but no electricity."

Hunter grabbed Morgan's arm theatrically. "Oh again? I can't wait."

"You don't have electricity?" Kevin asked, his eyes big.

"Well we didn't," Morgan said.

"Then you did?"

"No, then the house burned down, so now we really don't." Morgan grinned at him and he laughed a little, unsure of the joke. Mama made a small noise, and I looked at her.

"We aren't going to the house?" she asked.

"Sure aren't," Morgan said. "I guess maybe the fireplace survived, if you want to go see what you—"

"Why don't we get our rooms figured out," I interrupted. Morgan cut me a look and I stood my ground for once; maybe the painkiller made me foolishly brave.

"Oh yeah, sorry, here," Hunter produced a bouquet of keys. "I figure I'll bunk with Joyce, and Morgan and Allie are a team and I'll let the rest of you duke it out. Well. Kevin and Jason can't be in a room alone, that's a rule too."

"I'll be in a room with Kevin and Jason," Mama said.

"And me," Hunter repeated, still smiling. "We need everybody properly chaperoned of course, right Allie?" She winked at me and I blinked.

"Right," I said. Of course Mama and the boys weren't going to stay alone in a room, they wouldn't stay. Mama would call somebody and get us all rounded up. Some other, unforeseen betrayal in a long list of ones that maybe somebody should've seen coming.

"Alright, are we going to the restaurant like one big happy family or what?" Luke asked. I could almost be proud of him, for keeping to himself for so long and letting Morgan run the show, if I wasn't still so scared of him.

"Do you think we should do that?" I asked.

"Well I don't know about everybody else but I'm starving and want a beer, so I'm going to the restaurant. If more of you want to join me, you can do that." And he wandered off towards the restaurant, not looking back, Everett following.

"Man makes a good point," Morgan said.

"No, thank you," Mama said. "I'm exhausted from all of this and would prefer to go to sleep."

"Mama it's still light out," Kevin said.

"I don't recall asking you," she said.

"You…can go eat, Morgan," I said. "I'll stay with them."

"Nope, no can do, cuz," Morgan said. She still had her sunglasses on, or put them on again. "We'll just order room service."

"Well they don't do that," Hunter said, a laugh still in her voice. "But I'll go order and bring it back?"

"Perfect. See, we're problem solvers. Joe?"

"I'll eat with you, if that's okay?"

"It's fine," I said before Morgan could answer.

"Let's figure out what we're getting, then," Hunter said, letting us into one of the rooms. "Are you boys hungry, even if your Mama isn't?"

They looked at Mama for permission to be hungry, and she nodded slightly and set her purse down on the bed nearest the door.

"Sorry 'bout your deposit," Morgan said to Hunter, and went and yanked the phone cord out of the wall. The boys were shocked briefly into silence, huddling against me again, since Mama was being so quiet and cold.

"Well that probably could've been handled differently," Hunter said, then burst out laughing. "You're a maniac."

"Maybe I am." She dropped the cord on the floor, and then laughed and looked at Kevin and Jason. "Uh. Probably better you don't take my example."

Mama picked up her purse and moved it to the other bed, sat on the edge. It was the furthest she could be from us without standing in a corner. Her hands weren't folded, but she had that look in her eyes, and I knew she was praying.

"Ma'am, you don't have a cell phone, do you?" Hunter asked, in a far more civilized tone. In her fake-interviewer tone. Mama's eyes flicked to her and she shook her head. "Please tell me if you do. If those people come here, for you and the boys, they will hurt us."

"How dare you accuse me of lying," Mama said in a quiet voice, but a tone I'd never heard her use before. "The likes of *you*."

Hunter blinked, very surprised. She glanced at Morgan, whose back was to Mama, and I was glad because she was smiling. "I didn't say you were lying. I was just informing you of the risks."

"And now you're lying," Mama said, more strongly. "You monsters. All of you. I can tell from the look of you. Kevin, Jason, come over here." The boys obeyed, silent and big-eyed. "I hope they do come here and find us."

"Mama, you can't mean that," I said before I could stop myself. I saw Joe's head come around but I couldn't look at him. "How could you just leave me like that? Did you tell those people about us?"

"Of course I did." She was looking in her purse like she needed keys or a tissue or something. She just wanted to look anywhere but at me. Anywhere but at the monsters. "It was a way to be safe."

"From your sisters? What did they ever do to you?"

"They're monsters. Devils."

"You said that already. Then I'm a monster? A devil? Your own daughter?" She didn't say anything. "Mama, answer me."

"I had to be pregnant, I had to have a baby so he would take me away from them." She wouldn't look at me.

"What do you mean?" I crossed the room faster than I knew I could, grabbed her arm. "Mama, you mean Daddy..."

She twisted to get out of my gasp but I was too strong, and Jason started to cry, quietly. "He never touched me until we were married. I had you when I was sixteen." Was the gleam in her eyes tears or triumph?

"So then who was it? Who's my father?"

"We don't have fathers," she hissed and I let go of her then, fell back a step, at the hatred in her. "Satan. We're all the daughters of the Devil."

"Or God." We stared at each other across those few steps, her eyes burning into mine. "How dare you judge us like that. Nothing gives you the right."

I didn't know I was yelling, and or even what I said after that, just seeing red, but then Morgan was pulling me back. "Allie, much as I fuckin' love this, we can't have a noise complaint. Come on, let's take a walk. Come on."

I fought against her at first. I had the almost overwhelming impulse to hit her, and I think she would've understood, and let me get away with it just this once. But I stumbled away with her, the fight gone out of me just as fast as it had reared up. We got as far as the sidewalk out in front of the room doors and I sank down on the curb with my face in my hands. She tried to get me to get up, go someplace else, I don't know where, maybe the restaurant but I just couldn't and for once she couldn't budge me. Eventually, she stopped trying, and sat on the curb next to me.

We sat like that for a long time, or maybe it was only a little while, I couldn't tell. I couldn't really commit to crying, or stop crying, and just kind of panic-choked on that, angry and hurt and despairing. Mama really didn't want me, absolutely not anymore, and maybe not even in the first place. I imagined her leaving the house in the pines and going to the bowling alley that Morgan brought me to, meeting somebody who would, what, take her to the back of his car? To get pregnant so that the preacher she'd met would rescue her from her demon sisters. And mother, her mother was probably still alive then. Sixteen. That was when Morgan, probably the least comforting person in the world, put her arm around me.

"You gotta stop making that noise, people are gonna notice," she said quietly, roughly, but not mean. Not mean for once. I didn't know what noise I was making, but my throat hurt. My shoulder hurt. Everything hurt.

"What am I going to do?"

"You're gonna let Hunter take her and your brothers away to Betty and them, and then we're gonna fuck up Silvernail so bad that they say uncle and we don't have to worry about it ever again," she said steadily. "And you won't have to think about her anymore because she can't hurt you anymore. Not if you don't let her."

"Oh well if it's that easy." She laughed and rustled about with cigarettes and a lighter.

"Do you want one?" I raised my head and looked at her, at the offered pack. She'd never offered before; she knew what I'd say.

"No," I said. I'd never in my life wanted a cigarette, plus Mama was right inside and— "Yes."

She gave a little surprised head jerk, already taking the pack away to jam in her pocket, but she held it out again. I took one with my left hand, a little clumsily. I didn't know how I was supposed to hold it, or how to light it. Morgan watched me narrowly for a second, putting the pack away, then took my cigarette and put it in her mouth next to the first one, and lit both before handing one back to me. "You've never—"

"Of course I haven't." I sucked some air through it experimentally, listening to the paper crackle, filling my mouth with bitter smoke that I blew out immediately. Morgan took a drag, looking off across the parking lot, or into the middle distance, in her own thoughts or listening to whatever conversation they might be having in the room behind us. I couldn't hear anybody but my senses still weren't always reliable. I puffed again, experimentally. Maybe I was getting kind of a weird calm from the cigarette; Rachel smoked meditatively, not every day, maybe just one of a quiet evening. Morgan smoked either furiously or not at all. Nobody else in my life smoked before them, but they were the ones who had wanted me. Even Morgan, suddenly in charge of me with no warning, had seemed to only resent that I slowed her down, not that I existed. It was then that I took a deeper drag on the cigarette, actually inhaled, and coughed until I cried again.

"What's going on here?" Luke walked up while Morgan was cheerfully slapping me on the back. "You're just doing everything you can to corrupt her, aren't you?'

"Sure am," Morgan said with a grin. "And now it's finally working, so I'll thank you not to interrupt."

"Oh sorry, what was I thinking?" Luke looked at me then, because of course he'd only had eyes for Morgan. I didn't know what he saw in my face, but he looked back to Morgan and she shrugged. I looked at how much cigarette I had left and it was far more than I expected. I was very done but also didn't want to make Morgan mad at wasting it.

She reached over and took it. "Go get something to eat. Make Joe go with you."

"I'm not—"

"I don't care. Pretend I'm Dr. Fran if you gotta." She stood up, brushed off her jeans. "I'll even go get him for you, hold on."

"You don't need to—"

"Shut up, Allie." She brushed past Luke, putting her cigarette in his mouth before taking a drag off of mine. Startled, he turned with her as she passed and opened the room door. "Joe, come take Allie to dinner."

"Morgan."

"See? Simple. And just let me and Hunter take care of room assignments, okay?"

"Okay but—"

"Shut *up*, Allie." She was still grinning at me and Joe came outside, frowning a little.

"I guess they're ordering pizza?" he said, jerking his thumb over his shoulder at the room.

"The boys will like that," I said, standing up. I had a moment to wonder where Everett was, and then he slammed the truck door and crossed the parking lot with yet another laptop. Now the only person here we were hiding it from that Joyce was my Mama was Luke, and I didn't think it was all that good a secret.

"They're closing the restaurant soon," Everett said.

"Oh. Should we not go?" I didn't know what time it was. I never wore a watch, even back before all of this, when I was at home living a normal life.

"We can see if they'll still serve us," Joe said. "Or we can take a walk and see what's down the way, unless you're tired of fast food."

"I don't think Allie will ever get tired of fast food," Morgan said. "I know I haven't."

"And we're so much alike," I said, and when I laughed, and she laughed with me, I felt a little more normal. Grounded. So much of the time, recently, I've felt like the world was being yanked out from under me.

"Let's go then," Joe said.

"Be careful," Luke said, like it was an order.

"Yes sir."

# Chapter Five

O nce we were away from the hotel, Luke and Morgan still smoking out front, Everett gone into the room Hunter wasn't in with Mama and the boys, I couldn't really stand it anymore. "I guess if you have any questions, we should get that out of the way," I said.

"I think I've pieced things together pretty well," Joe said in a slow, careful tone. Like it was as true a statement as he could make, but he didn't mean anything bad by it. "I'm sorry."

"Thank you." I paused a second, but somehow, my emotions had smoothed out again. I was still sad and nervous, but that was just how I felt a lot lately. "I wanted to say something, when you told me that your dad—"

"No, it's okay. I understand why you wouldn't."

"Though also I feel like an idiot, because all you need to do is look at us. Of course Luke knows too, now. Or has an idea."

"Probably," he agreed. I was a little surprised at how quiet it was here. Wasn't this a town? But when we walked away from the hotel, we were on a broad, long stretch of road with street lights but no houses, and a grocery store, and a gas station lighting up the distance next to a McDonald's. "But Luke doesn't know the whole of it, and we're going to be done with this part soon enough. Oh that sounds bad, I'm sorry."

"But no, you're right. We'll be done." I'd thought or hoped I was done, that I might never see Mama again anyway, and yet here we were. Maybe after this, was when I would never see her again. "Hunter's taking them off tomorrow, and we're going on to whatever it is your family has planned for taking the initiative instead of waiting around to be ambushed again. We won't be worrying about them anymore."

"Exactly."

"Did today seem to go too easy?" I asked suddenly.

He scratched the back of his head. "Too easy how?"

"For the, uh, mission part of it, anyway. Nothing went wrong? We had a plan, we did the plan and now we're here. We didn't even get a flat tire. Nothing." Well not until Mama called us all monsters and told me that she got pregnant from just anybody she could find so that Daddy would take her away from home. Though Rachel told me once that it never mattered who our fathers were, Culvers were just Culvers.

"I think they weren't expecting you to have help. They weren't expecting you to leave the Jeep."

"I guess." I shouldn't borrow trouble, I definitely had enough of my own. But I felt that little bite of rising dread in the pit of my stomach. "You don't think they let us go on purpose, to track them?"

Joe reached like he was going to put a hand on my arm to comfort me, stopped himself. I was glad he did, but also glad he thought of it. "I don't think that, no. And Everett already checked stuff for bugs."

"He did?" I didn't remember that. But he was in the back of the truck with Morgan, right behind Mama and the boys. He could have checked, however he did, from there and nobody would've known.

"Yeah, he was worried about that. It's his job to worry about that kind of stuff. But no, I think they really just didn't know how to anticipate what you would do instead of sticking to their meetup idea."

"Okay good."

"If we were at home and Grandpa was debriefing, he'd say 'today was a good day.'"

"Would he?" I didn't remember Bill Ward saying that at any point. Maybe none of our debriefs were on good days. That tracked.

We got into the McDonald's right before it closed everything but the drive thru, got milkshakes and chicken nuggets and french fries. "So it really surprises me that Morgan would like vanilla milkshakes," Joe said as we walked back.

"I was surprised too, but she really does." It was also what I'd gotten. "We don't really like chocolate."

"No, me neither. Strawberry, though."

"It's okay. Not as good as vanilla, maybe, but it's okay." He wrinkled his nose and I laughed, maybe surprised that I felt like teasing anybody, much less Joe Ward.

Back at the hotel, nobody was outside anymore, and most of the rooms were dark. I hadn't paid attention to how many cars were in the parking lot, but it wasn't very many. Maybe that was a reason Hunter picked this place, in addition to her dedication to the aesthetic. No tourist attractions to really draw crowds, even though it was getting to be summer. Maybe it was a popular place for people hunting on weekends. I remembered Daddy doing that sometimes, going hunting, and my breath got caught for a second.

Joe looked at his phone for longer than he needed to, and then said, "I don't know what rooms we're supposed to be in," he said. "Nobody texted me."

I finished my milkshake, straw rattling in the bottom, and started to get my phone out, but Morgan appeared as if summoned, her braid undone. "Hey, we put your stuff in this room, here's the key," she said.

"Both of our stuff?" Joe asked.

"Yeah. Problem?" She wasn't grinning, wasn't laughing. I wondered if Mama had continued her performance and thought that I probably couldn't make myself go back into a room with her unless it was life or death. Then I realized that might well happen, the way things were going.

"It's fine," I said. "There's two beds, it's fine."

"You're sure?" Joe asked.

"Yeah, it's okay."

"Perfect." We got a flash of teeth then. It wasn't even super late, but I was so tired after everything today. Probably everybody else was too.

"Goodnight, cuz," I said, and her eyes caught the streetlights for a second. I didn't know what she was up to, but even when I didn't trust Morgan, I had to trust Morgan. She always had some internal logic, some plan that would make sense at its conclusion.

"Goodnight," she said. "Don't do anything I wouldn't do."

I laughed, loud and surprised. "I think that's impossible." Except for the one thing, but it was already done. *Mama, I can't.* She just shook her head and walked back up the way, laughing a little.

I got changed in the bathroom and then crawled into my bed while Joe got changed. I imagined Hunter and Morgan keeping Mama and the boys under watch. Maybe they were taking turns staying awake, so Mama wouldn't do anything. Any other time, maybe I'd be worried about sharing a room just me and Joe, but instead of worrying or even thinking much more at all, I fell asleep before he even finished in the bath-room.

When I opened my eyes again, it was like no time had passed at all and also like I'd slept for a million years. What woke me up? Joe was breathing deeply and evenly in the next bed. Then I heard the scuff of boots on the gravel out front and I thought, oh no they tracked us after all. Was it better to wake Joe up or not.

I was on my feet and to the door before I realized no, it was Morgan and Hunter. It was Hunter's steps I didn't recognize, but Morgan's gait I knew, even in my sleep. Even with the limp. They were arguing quietly about something and both looked at me at the same time when I opened the room door.

"You're up early," Hunter said.

"So are you."

"Are we gonna have to feed these kids before they get on the road?" Morgan asked.

"They don't like eating in the morning," I said. That was true, or it used to be true. Could that much have changed in less than a year?

"Fair enough." Morgan couldn't understand not being hungry.

"What's going on?" Joe said behind me.

"Just Morgan and Hunter sneaking around," I said. "God knows why."

"Maybe we wanted some time to ourselves," Hunter said, shaking her head.

"Wait, if you're out here, who's with—"

"Luke and Everett," Morgan said. "Look we might *seem* ir-responsible but we aren't actually irresponsible."

Hunter swatted at her. "I do not seem irresponsible."

"Next to Allie you do."

"Well next to Allie we're all just the worst."

"Oh come on," I said, shifting uneasily.

"Anyway, Hunter's gonna head out soon with Joyce and the boys, and we're gonna head to Bill's to see what the next step is. So be ready...uh...soon anyway."

"Okay," I said, and Joe echoed me, shuffling off to the bathroom. "How was it last night?"

Morgan snickered and Hunter looked at me with her eyebrows raised. "How was what? Morgan, stop. Oh, how'd your Mama behave. It was okay, she mostly prayed. She let the boys gorge themselves on pizza and then watch cartoons until they passed out. They said grace over pizza, is that normal? I'm sorry, I know it's rude, but that doesn't seem normal."

"For Mama? Yes. We always said grace." If you didn't, there'd be hell to pay. In a lot of ways, in most ways, I never missed Mama at all, I didn't know why I was so upset now. Maybe because I wanted to be the one to reject her, not the other way around. "I'll be ready soon."

"Roger that," Morgan said, loud enough for the Wards to hear, presumably, and Hunter laughed again.

Joe had already gotten dressed, somehow, and was brushing his teeth. "I'll be out in a second," he mumbled.

"It's okay." I would never ask him, but he'd told me about his dad and never mentioned his mom. Maybe she couldn't stand all the Wards' military and quasi military stuff and she left. Or maybe she just didn't keep Joe's dad from making him leave home. That wasn't something that was forgivable, I didn't think. Maybe I was just never a good enough Christian; that's definitely what Mama always thought, and I never knew why until now. I didn't have any way to be a good enough Christian for Mama, and she was never going to love me the way she loved the boys.

Once I was ready, I hesitated at the door. Joe had already gone out, taking our stuff to the truck. I could hear Hunter and Morgan in the parking lot, talking about the car Hunter had, which was not the vehicle she would have for Morgan, that would be something different. Morgan's voice raised for a moment. "No Hunter, I do not want a fucking Bronco. No."

"But the new ones are cute," Hunter protested. "And have *four* doors! And—"

"Nope."

"Fine." Hunter was laughing a little and Morgan wasn't.

I thought, I don't need to go out there and see Mama again. It was enough that we did this, and she didn't want to see me, after all. But the boys would, or they'd think they did. That and the break in Morgan and Hunter's argument was what got me out of the room, in time to walk them to the car. Mama trailed behind, not wanting to get too close to me and definitely not wanting to let the boys alone with me.

"You be good for Hunter now, okay? She's a really good friend." Honestly, if they were bad for Hunter, I'd expect she'd eat them alive.

"Why aren't you coming, Allie?" Jason asked.

"Well I've got to go someplace else, I'm sorry." I made myself smile at him, what I thought might be my old smile. My 'trying to be good for Mama and Daddy' smile. My big sister smile. "But I'll see you again."

"Mama and Daddy never talked about you after you left," Kevin said. "And I got your room."

"But you two weren't going to share a room forever," I said evenly. "It only makes sense that you'd get my room."

"Were you really on mission? Why didn't you write to us?" Jason asked plaintively. "We never get any mail."

"I'm sorry, guys. I just wasn't where I could send mail. I'll try to do it once you're settled, though."

"Will you?" Kevin asked.

"Cross my heart." Was I lying to him? I didn't know. But I hugged them both as tight as I was able, which wasn't enough, and they got into Hunter's car, a convertible Range Rover. I didn't know they made convertible Range Rovers.

"Why isn't Daddy here?" Kevin asked suddenly, right as I was closing the door.

"Well I guess you'll have to talk to Mama about that," I said, forcing another smile. "Bye, I'll miss you."

"Bye Allie," they chorused, and I shut the door and stepped away. Mama stood staring at me when I turned around.

"Alleluia," she said, and I shook my head.

"Look. Let Hunter take you and the boys to Betty. Build a new life. When they're old enough, sixteen, seventeen, whatever, you tell them how to find me. And if they don't within a couple years of that, I'll come looking for you, and you don't want that." I paused. I didn't know why Betty would agree to this, actually. But I didn't need to tell Mama that. "And if they change, you better find me sooner."

She gave a little sniff, and walked past me, back rigid, to get in the car. She didn't look at me again, but the boys waved, and

I waved back at them as Hunter hopped into the car, tooted once, and drove off.

I smelled Morgan behind me before she said anything. "Think she will?"

"What, tell the boys where to find me? Yeah, I think so."

"If she doesn't?"

"I meant what I said." If we live through this, I didn't say.

• • • •

I WAS SURPRISED AT how happy Bill seemed to be when we pulled up at the latest cabin headquarters. That just hadn't been mine and Morgan's experience with him, to date. "How'd it go?" he asked from the porch.

"About how you'd expect," Luke said, shrugging. "No action, no tail." Everett nodded to confirm.

"A good day," Bill said, and I snuck a look at Joe, who was looking at me. He raised his eyebrows like 'see?' and I smiled. "Does anybody need seeing to?"

"Allie, probably," Morgan said, shocking me with her betrayal. She'd been suspiciously quiet for the drive, even dozing off at points. I guess we'd spent a few too many days not getting enough sleep. Even though I'd never known Morgan to get enough sleep, except when drugged.

"I'm fine," I said. I was in pain, but that was to be expected. I'd worn my sling for the drive, that helped.

"You're not." She smiled sweetly.

"We need you operational, so let's get on with it," Bill said. I stared at Morgan, because I couldn't imagine what she was pulling, but she pretended not to see, walking off with Luke and Everett in the direction the coffee smells were coming from.

"I should be saying thank you," I said. "I'm sorry."

"It's nothing to worry about." He had an unsmoked cigar in his shirt pocket with a little spiral bound notebook, and I thought he seemed different from when we first met him, at that club. He seemed more engaged now, with this big project to focus on. This operation. Maybe he'd been bored. Maybe he was just invested in the promise of more grandkids.

"How is Mrs. Ward?" I asked, because it was polite and because I wasn't comfortable with the silence, exactly, as he led me through the cabin to whoever the medic was.

"She's furious and staying with her sister," he said with a chuckle. "How is Rachel? I sort of expected—"

"Oh, she disowned us," I said after a horrified moment where I wished Luke had already filled Bill in on some things so that I wouldn't have to. I tried on one of Morgan's tone of voice, flinty and honest and not inviting further questions. It didn't really suit me too well.

"We knew she didn't want any involvement, after what happened to you on that diner outing. But you pushed that envelope, didn't you?" He looked at me; he'd caught my tone. He didn't care.

I made it a point to stare back. It was me, and it was Morgan. "Sure did."

"Anyway, you were right all along that it's a bigger problem than a Culver problem, and we've put out feelers and had at least one other family express interest in working together."

"That's good news." Put out feelers how, I wondered? Through the Coutards? Not through Rachel.

"It is. Okay, Ezra was there when we pulled Sela out of that first facility, I don't know if you remember." The bedroom probably wasn't always a sickbay, but it was a good space for it, with a long low table to have instruments and supplies laid out on.

"I do. I just didn't catch his name then." I managed to find a friendly enough smile. "Thanks for helping me out."

"It's kind of selfish," he said. "I've never seen a silver bullet hole."

"I'm just a curiosity, I get it," I said, and we all laughed a little. Bill left then, striding off to marshall his army or whatever. Organize the guerillas. Ezra and I looked at each other for a second and I hesitated and then said, "I can't really lift my arm enough to get my shirt off."

"I should've thought of that, sorry." He helped me with the sling and my shirt, and he had a very light touch, reminding me of any nurse I'd ever seen in my life, and I relaxed a little. "Okay, despite everything, this is looking pretty good. We'd like to see more progress on your collarbone, you need to keep wearing the sling and keep your activity down."

"You know that I can't really do that right now," I said, thinking of last winter and trying to keep Morgan as couch and bed ridden as possible so that she would heal up and not end up with a worse limp than what she had. The ideal would've been no limp, but I didn't think any of us believed that dream would come true. Dulcie might have, if we still had her.

"I do know that. But I also know that some of your family is sitting this out." So they did already know, and Bill made me say it to him out of pure meanness. An early reminder of what dealing with the Wards was like. Everything was just test after test to see what anybody could handle. To feel out limits, and boundaries.

I lifted my chin. "They are. And I'm not."

He nodded, because of course that was what I was going to say. "Suit yourself." He helped me put my shirt back on, gave me a bottle without a label half full of painkillers. "Maybe see about getting yourself some button downs, I'm surprised nobody thought of it before now."

"We've had a lot going on. And it's summer."

"You can cut the sleeves off."

"Thanks," I said, and went to find Morgan.

"Hunter just texted me," she said. She was partway through a beer already. "They made good time."

"Wow, yeah they did." I looked in the nearby coolers; beer in the first one, sodas in the second, bottled water in the third, and that's what I picked. Then I realized I couldn't open it one handed, and started to put it back when Morgan said

"Give it here. Jesus, you're stubborn." She finished her beer and dropped it in a nearby bin, took the cap off my water.

# Chapter Six

For all the testing and the 'can you handle this' and 'are you sure you want to do this' talk, there wasn't any doing for a week after that. It wasn't relaxing; it was a calm before a storm, with equipment checks, mini briefings, some rudimentary firing range action. Morgan was itching both because she wanted to *do* something and also because, without a vehicle, we were just stuck here at the Wards' behest. In some ways I didn't mind that, because it meant I didn't have to anticipate her ramming off either, and making me a participant. I was able to actually rest for once, and feel like I was healing.

In other ways, yeah, it wasn't a great feeling.

But it was physical rest I needed, even though I didn't fool myself that anybody was doing it on my behalf. Bill Ward just didn't like rushing into anything, even though he'd decided he was going to do it. They had extended war room sessions, for anybody there that wanted to sit in, talking strategy and structure. Morgan went to them a lot, probably more than they wanted her to, and I sat out a lot, because all I wanted to know was what we were doing and when. I couldn't worry about anything beyond that; I wasn't a planner, I wasn't a strategist, I wasn't a leader. I didn't want to be any of those things.

Sometimes the Wards went on a wolf run in the early mornings or evenings and Morgan went with them. I'd sit on the porch and listen to them, and pretend that I could tell everybody's individual strides. Morgan's I could. I was starting to think that I knew Joe's. But Luke and the other bigger, heavier guys all blended together.

Sometimes she didn't go, and sat on the porch with me, or inside, with one of the acoustic guitars and noodled around, in parts like she wanted and craved the practice and other times like it genuinely helped her think. In some ways, Morgan was just accepted into the fold. She was like one of the guys, like Luke said to me in Tyler's kitchen months and months ago, that scary night. They mostly left me alone, which I liked just fine, but when they didn't leave me alone they were surprisingly nice. Asked if I needed anything. Told me what dinner was. Said if somebody was going into town, but that only happened once.

"Hey play Freebird," Luke said one afternoon, stepping outside and lighting a cigarette.

"You're such a fuckin' grandpa," she said, looking up at him and holding out her hand. He handed her the cigarette and she took a drag, handed it back. Then she strummed a few bars. "It'd be better on the electric, except I lost my slide someplace. I'd have to use a beer bottle or something."

Luke looked at me questioningly and I shook my head. "I didn't know you could do that either, no."

"Me personally, or in general?"

"Yes."

"I don't know anything about music," Luke said.

"Well you're in luck, because I'm not gonna teach you anything."

He laughed. "Well thanks."

"No problem." She looked at me. "What about you, any requests?"

"You've never asked me that before," I said, surprised. Her train of thought really must've gotten derailed. The fact that she asked me made my mind just go blank. "I don't know."

"You two are so boring. *Everett*." She could get so loud so suddenly, without any discernible windup.

From somewhere inside, he yelled back "*Yeah?*"

"Song request?"

A pause. "Killing in the Name."

Luke laughed. "Well now you definitely need the electric."

"Actually, I don't," she said smugly.

"What, do you just not know it? The biggest literal fuck you song?"

"Didn't say that." She plucked her fourth string and sixth together, and let them ring as she tuned the sixth string down. "It helps to always be able to do the unexpected."

"I can tell that's your motto."

Instead of answering him, she struck a chord, bobbed her head slightly in a count, did it again. "Gonna sing for me?" she asked the porch in general and I shook my head because I absolutely did not know this song and Luke laughed again.

"You don't want that."

"Having a hell of a time putting a band together," she said to me while playing a sort of frenetic riff. I still didn't recognize the song.

"You *have* a band."

"Yeah but I feel like I'm probably going to outgrow them. Or did outgrow them. We'll see what happens when we get back together after all this." The song had changed to a kind of walking melody. Everett had appeared just inside the screen door.

"You should put that on your acoustic covers album," I said.

"You haven't even heard me sing it yet." She stopped, muted the strings with her hand. "I won't sully your ears with such crass lyrics right now."

"Damn," Everett said.

"I keep forgetting you're a fan."

Luke stubbed out his cigarette, dropped it in the bucket they had on the porch. "Wait, Everett, you knew who this maniac was before all this?"

"I knew her music, yeah. I didn't realize that's who she was right away." It was hard to see Everett's face, whether he was embarrassed or just apprehensive.

"How did you not know? How many Morgan Culvers are in the world, do you figure?" Luke leaned against the porch rail, folding his arms.

"I didn't think about it, we were all kind of focused. Plus her hair's different."

"The hair is a big one," Morgan said. "Well you saw it. I bleach the top white and straighten it, for shows and interviews and whatever. For when I'm operating as a rock star in public. It sounds like a tiny little change, but apparently it makes a huge difference." I'd forgotten that Morgan dyed her hair back to black the night we rescued Sela.

"Oh yeah, I forgot."

"How could you forget?" Everett asked, in that same sarcastic tone.

"There's been a lot going on," Luke said easily, and they laughed. "Anyway you were right to drop the bleached look for this."

"Just as good a disguise as sunglasses, except I wear 'em too often for them to be a disguise."

"Maybe you need a hat," I said, to feel like I was involved.

"Ooh yeah, what kind do you think? Baseball cap? Cowboy hat?"

"I think a cowboy hat would draw more attention than you'd want a disguise to," Everett said.

"It probably would. Plus, it'd be misleading. Musically speaking." She'd started noodling with the guitar again while we were talking, something perkier and fingerpick-y that I did know; I remembered, I told her that I knew how to play "Landslide," when I was in the back of the Jeep after getting shot, and she was distracting me, maybe while Hunter pulled a piece of silver out of my skin. This was "Never Going Back Again." But no, she wasn't going to make me sing in front of Luke Ward. "Come on, Allie."

"No, thank you."

She rolled her eyes and stopped playing again. "There's only so much I can carry a crowd," she said, pulling the guitar case over. "And this one isn't even paying me."

"You want me to pay you? I think I have a twenty." Luke reached for his wallet. He wasn't smiling, but there was that particular look in his eyes.

"No, that wasn't the point. But who knows, maybe one day a private twenty dollar concert could be yours."

Somebody in the cabin called Everett, and he went away again. Luke cocked his head to listen, and then lit another cigarette. "Bored out of my fucking skull," he said conversationally, offering the pack to us. Morgan took one.

"Glad I'm not the only one," Morgan said, leaning over for him to light her cigarette. "Who knew you'd have gone so hard for homebrew bureaucracy."

"That's all Bill, and it makes enough sense to keep the rest of us knuckleheads in line." Weird that Luke never called Bill anything but his first name; much like how Morgan almost always called Rachel by her first name. With Luke, it seemed more like an operational thing. If everybody was first names there was no way to know how anybody was related to each other. With Morgan, I could only assume it was just another boundary to be tested.

"Bill, plus you all going into the military and getting brainwashed."

"We're not all cut out for fame and fortune."

Morgan barked a laugh and a cloud of smoke. "Truer words have rarely been spoken."

Everett came back to the door. "Okay, we're getting some assignments."

"Praise Jesus, It's about fucking time," Morgan said.

We gathered in a room that had a big long wooden table in it. I could imagine all of the Wards cramming around for a holiday dinner, laughing and talking and bickering. Bill stood at the head of it and Luke went and stood with him. I glanced at Joe, wondering what this would be like for him if his dad was here, standing on the other side of Bill. How many more sons did Bill have? No matter.

"This is a war we should've started a long time ago and now we have to play catch up," he started. "We might not have the same level of resources, but Silvernail doesn't know that. They only know who a few of us are, and they only know where some of us are. They don't know our numbers, our organization, our resources. The way we make them stop? We don't stop. We hit a clinic. We burn a car. We don't have an army, truly, and we don't have a battlefield. So we stage a guerilla war. We have sufficient intel on them, it's just a matter of how we use it. All their clinic locations, lab locations, executive suites. Names of shareholders, employee names."

Morgan fidgeted next to me. We all knew all this, what was the point in a speech? She saw me looking and made a face.

"So the techies are mostly going to be staying at bases to see what they can do to hit them from that angle, and we'll hand out assignments like we did in Georgia. Keep them compartmentalized; if one of us gets grabbed, the less each one of you knows about the broader op, the better." He chuckled. "And so when I say that we've got a secure server that we're trying to on-board families, it sounds like I'm directly contradicting myself, but there it is." Some tense laughter rippled through the room, but the excitement was palpable. There'd never been anything like this. No reason for the families to unite. Other than the supposed Coutard get-togethers I'd heard mentioned, which were handshake events at best, everybody was antisocial. And with good reason, probably maybe, but this was a big enough threat, even though it was sort of a small company, all things considered. Fertility clinics and some associated drugs and research. That was it, that was all Silvernail was. But they had so much money, just from that, and that's where all the private security came in.

Maybe the one who liked to shoot with silver and burn things was part of *that* family, I thought suddenly. Maybe they couldn't bear the idea of us monsters just out here living like people, and their own personal mission was getting us under their control. So they could use us for super soldiers and whatever other gene splicing and designer babies they were interested in. Maybe there really had been a reason, once, the family was named Silvernail.

While I was woolgathering, Morgan was getting our assignment, but that was probably for the better anyway. "Me and you and Luke and Joe are a team," she said, coming back.

"I guess that makes sense."

"Yeah, we'll have to see if they can keep up," she said, grinning at Luke, who seemed to have caught her last statement.

"What are we doing? Uh. Our mission?"

"We'll talk about it in the truck," Luke said.

"Are we leaving now?" I asked. I didn't know why I was surprised.

"I'll get our stuff, Allie, just get yourself to the truck," Morgan said.

It was either a kindness or a detriment that they were letting me participate at all, I didn't know which I thought yet. I made my way out to the driveway, found Luke's truck.

"This is going to be weird without Everett," Joe said as he came up behind me, clearly careful to make sure I heard him and he wasn't sneaking.

"It is, you're right. But it was already weird to have more than me and Morgan, so I guess we'll adjust."

"That's true, it's always been you and Morgan." He wasn't right, exactly, but he was right enough. A lot of this wasn't real until it was me and Morgan. "Wonder if Hunter found her a new car or Jeep or whatever yet. You'd have to figure a Jeep, right?"

"I'd expect, yeah. Hunter's kind of funny, though."

"That she is."

"What're you saying about Hunter?" Morgan asked, startling me so badly that I let out a weird little noise that seemed to startle *her*.

"Wondering what your new wheels would be," Joe said.

"Oh, that. Yeah I don't know yet either." She gave me a side-long glance. "You gonna make it?"

"Just should've realized that the kid gloves were off," I said. "It's about time things went back to normal around here."

"Exactly what I was thinking," she said, grinning wickedly. "Alrighty, want to get in there and hotwire this before—"

"Please don't fucking hotwire my truck, come on. I'm right here." I could almost pity Luke for having to suffer Morgan. Almost.

They stowed the bags and we got on the road.

"So what's on the docket?" Morgan asked after not much time.

"Good old-fashioned arson," Luke said, glancing at her in the rear view. "Which we might need some gas for, I'm not sure."

"Oh, is that all?" Morgan said, not looking at me. "Piece of cake."

"No casualties," Joe said, probably smelling whatever it is that I give off when my stomach drops.

"The rules of engagement?" Morgan asked archly.

"The rules of the engagement. Though we know how those can change," Luke said, looking at her in his mirror again.

"Don't we, though." She was drumming her fingertips on the armrest, looking out the window.

We didn't really know what to talk about, us and the Wards. Luke still scared me more than a little, and even though he wasn't being quite so mean to Joe anymore, Joe didn't seem super comfortable with him either. Morgan was the only one who was never uncomfortable, ever, and she sometimes talked, sometimes didn't, dragging us along with her train of thought.

Joe and I never ended up even seeing the warehouse. Luke stopped for the gas, and then parked a couple of miles away and he and Morgan got out. "It's best if only a couple of us go," Luke said. "That way they don't get all of us if they're ready for us."

"They won't be ready," Morgan said.

"Still and all..."

"I'm fine staying in the truck," I said. They were being easy on me, or didn't want me in the way, and I was more than happy to go along with that. Joe nodded, moving over to the driver's seat. I scrunched down in the back, so that it wouldn't look like we were a couple of people just kind of loitering there, but maybe just one driver waiting for something. Somebody. Morgan left me her phone while she was gone, and the very act of her handing it over was just shocking. It didn't buzz the entire time, no texts or calls or anything, and I just held it in front of me in both hands like it was a talisman or something. I guess I never really thought about how much Morgan did or didn't trust me, starting with when we had to work together because it was her and me and that was it, right up to the present.

They came back at a far more leisurely pace than I would've expected, but that was far less suspicious, wasn't it. Morgan slid in next to me, Luke got in the passenger seat. They smelled like gasoline and matches, not enough that a normal person would notice it but I sure did. "Start driving," Luke said. "Just a nice, normal, at the speed limit pace. There's gonna be a boom pretty soon, but I think we're probably already outside of the immediate range of suspicion."

"I didn't actually see any cameras," Morgan said. I handed over her phone before she even asked for it.

"A boom?" I asked.

"They had some conveniently placed propane tanks," Luke said. "And liquid nitrogen, God knows what that was for, medical shit I guess. It's almost like they wanted us to blow that place up, but the supplies have been there for months, Everett says."

"Weird," I said, mystified. But what else could I say? "Not everybody was just going to out of the way warehouses, though."

"No, they weren't. But that's a need to know—"

Morgan gave a short, impatient laugh. "Christ, enough with that. Maybe you're washed-up military but we aren't, talk like normal." I heard Joe's hands tighten on the steering wheel, and it got very quiet in the truck. Luke, in the seat in front of me, didn't say anything, and I listened to his breathing give a short hitch. Was he hurt? Surprised? I didn't understand how he could be. We were away from whatever little town that was when I felt the boom, almost subsonically, more than hearing it. I turned around and looked out the back windshield, and a dark stream of smoke was beginning to rise past the rooftops. "There she blows," Morgan said, grinning.

We drove on in silence for I didn't know how long, probably not very, but I couldn't stand it. "What's next?" I asked.

"Are you so eager for action?" Luke asked.

"No, she just wants to get it over with," Morgan said. "I'm out of cigarettes, how about we stop."

"Not yet," he growled.

"Sure, sure." She slouched down in her seat, her face lit by her phone screen. She laughed almost inaudibly. "Oh. Well that's timing for you."

"What is it now?" Luke turned partway around.

"Hold on, the service on this phone is shit, I'm waiting for the picture to load." We all waited. "Okay, Hunter saw this in a tabloid." She held out the phone and as I started to look at it, Luke reached over and took it.

"'Where's Morgan? We asked the members of Howling when we could expect to see them play again,'" he read out loud. "One, I still can't believe that's what your band is named."

"Like it or not, it is what it is," Morgan said. "And there are plenty of regular old people with far more wolfy band names. They aren't nearly as good, by the way."

"Of course not. But for fucking two, they know who you are?" He handed the phone back, and this time I grabbed it. One of the band members in the grainy picture was the guy who made my fake ID. The bass player. Al? I think Al.

"Weren't we just talking about my striking appearance? But yeah, we knew that. It's perfect, isn't it?"

"You *knew* that." He wasn't asking. Morgan ignored him, looking at me, her eyes catching the streetlights.

"Why is it perfect?" I asked finally, to keep Luke from un-buckling his seatbelt and coming into the backseat to strangle her.

"I'll be bait. We've been worried about them tracking us, slap a tracker on me. I'll go on the morning show or some shit.

NPR! Wait no they've got a super long lead time, the bastards. Still, there's a business model for it, it's fine. Why didn't we think of this sooner?"

Luke said "I don't know if that's the best—"

"Nobody fuckin' asked you. So we'll have them take me to whatever the new people stealing facility is, and you follow and—"

"That isn't the plan."

"Luke, I don't *care*. What's your better plan? In the long term? There's only so much of this we're going to do before getting too much attention, fun as it is. They like taking people, we let them take a people. Or we could take one of their people, you wanna do that? One of the young Silvernail heiresses, you got the stomach for that, Luke Ward? Shut the fuck up. You're not as cold-blooded as you want us to think."

He was quiet for a minute and then said, "Bill floated that idea."

"Well good, because from the score I've been keeping, we're a little behind on that. Also body count but just by one." I flinched and she cut her eyes to me. "And you're not as cold blooded as any of us, Allie, it's fine. We know."

"I—"

"No it's good, stay gold, never change. Now pull over someplace so I can go call my manager. This isn't going to be an instant thing, we can keep going with our little missions first. Really get them riled up and that way the target's clearly painted."

Joe kept driving, and then hesitantly asked, "Are we really going to let her do this?"

"Nobody 'lets' Morgan do anything," I said, before she could take his head off.

"Yeah, don't act like that statement doesn't also apply to you," Luke said with a short laugh.

"What? I don't—"

"You already always go along with her plans, but you've had at least one of your own. Was it Morgan who taught you how to hotwire a car?"

"Yes." I didn't need to explain myself to him, I thought, and I guess that really only proved his point, because he started to say something else and Morgan cut him off.

"Leave Allie alone. Are we gonna pull over or what?"

"I was looking for a place that would have cigarettes too," Joe said. He was also waiting for Luke to give him the okay, I was sure, but he didn't say that part.

"Okay," Morgan said, as we drove past a convenience store. "What was wrong with that one?"

"Cop out front," Joe said, keeping his eyes straight ahead, and I turned around to see if that was true but there were trees. Maybe Joe was just a better liar than me. Everybody was a better liar than me.

"Joe unless you want to see my neat trick where I tuck and roll while exiting a moving vehicle..."

"Stop up here," Luke said. "And I'll call to get the go-ahead. And about what kind of tracker we can get."

"Oh, aye aye sir," Morgan said. She started to salute and then let her hand fall, cocking her head. "Do you salute, in the Navy? Did you?"

"Yes," Luke said, after a pause. Probably weighing the consequences of engaging.

They needed to sort out their rules of engagement, I thought, and then couldn't help myself and a laugh slipped out. Morgan looked at me curiously and that made me laugh more. Normal laughter, I didn't feel hysterical or upset or like I couldn't stop. The only thing that was weird about it was I was the only one.

"I just can't," I said. "I'm sorry."

"You just don't normally laugh like that." She was laughing now too.

"I know."

Joe looked at us in the mirror, smiling a little but also confused. Luke stayed staring straight ahead. We pulled over at a twenty four hour convenience store, big yellow lights at the edges of the parking lot with halos of early summer bugs looping around them. Morgan hopped out and was already dialing. Luke didn't get out of the truck, just tapped a couple things and was ringing through to Bill, I assumed. Joe looked at me and tilted his head towards the store, and I nodded and we got out of the truck. I could feel Luke watching us go, and Morgan's laugh cut through the night as the automatic doors swooshed open.

"We seem to be making a habit of this," I said as we were pouring coffees.

"A habit of what?"

"Going away to a store or something while the grownups are talking."

"We're not *not* grownups," Joe said. Morgan had even said so, pretty recently. Then he looked at me. "Oh."

"I'm *close*," I said. I didn't know why I was in such a hurry to be a grownup; I knew the Culver problem. And the Culver problem was probably a big part of why Morgan was the way she was.

"Close enough that we should be getting you a birthday present or?"

"No, February."

"Plenty of time," he said. Were we flirting? Oh I thought maybe he was trying to flirt gently. Oh what did I do about that?

The doors swooshed open again and we both looked at Luke walking in. He took the store in at a glance, nobody here but us werewolves and the clerk, and he went to the counter to buy cigarettes. That was the level of Luke's regard that I was more comfortable with, which was to say, not really paying attention to me. When I looked back to Joe, he had kind of the same look on his face.

"Do you think he'll get Morgan's cigarettes too?" I asked, and he shrugged.

"If he's feeling generous."

Luke heard us, of course, smirked slightly. We got in line behind him and he said, "Their stuff too. Joe, get me the biggest coffee? Just black. Thanks." And he stalked off to the bathrooms at the back, leaving some bills on the counter. The clerk looked at us and shrugged.

"Did that just happen?" Joe asked.

"Sure did," I said. I looked out the door for Morgan, but she wasn't in the first puddle of lights, and the glare of night kept her invisible. I didn't like not being able to see her, not because I was worried for her safety, but because I was worried about what she might be doing. But she always walked around on the phone, wrote notes on her hands and arms, who even knew what else she might get up to.

Luke came back up front, collected his change and his coffee. "Are we ready?" he asked.

"Morgan hasn't come in yet."

"You sure she isn't back at the truck?"

"I didn't check." It never occurred to me she'd just go back to the truck.

He laughed. "Afraid of the dark?"

"Not when you're not in it," I said, and went outside. It wasn't the parting shot that I thought it was, of course, and I nearly ran into Morgan when she came around the corner from behind the ice machine.

"Well that took fuckin' forever and he'll still have to call me back, of course."

"You fell off the face of the earth for awhile, you have to figure that—"

"That isn't *new*. Oh, did you see? Do they have that paper here, with the interview?"

"No, I didn't think to look." I should have. I turned around to go back inside and Luke was coming out.

"Got you cigarettes," he said a little gruffly, tossing Morgan the pack.

"Thank you," she said, seeming genuinely surprised. "Gimme five and I'll be out. Allie, wait for me?"

"Okay." Joe was gone already with my coffee, so I looked for the newspapers while Morgan did her thing. Hunter's picture hadn't included what paper it was, but when I found something a little less news-y but not quite tabloid, I thought I was on the right track, and flipped a couple of pages in until I found it. I picked up one copy, and then gathered two more. No sense getting just one.

"Did you find it? Did we all get coffee? What's the plan?" She appeared next to me, wiping her hands on her jeans. Which probably meant that she didn't just appear, and I was either very tired or in pain again, or both.

"Yes, yes, and I don't know. It's late." Meaning, we were probably going to stop somewhere. Meaning, I didn't know how useful I could be for much longer, which was a little joke anyway, because we'd debated my usefulness more than once to begin with.

"Well that's pretty good, though. I'm surprised Luke got me the cigarettes, think he's keeping score?"

"I'd be shocked if he wasn't."

"Yeah, me too." She looked at the coffee options and got a giant vanilla cappuccino from the machine. It had to come powdered like hot chocolate, I thought. It smelled so sweet. I wanted to ask about her phone call, since her arms were conspicuously free from pen, but I for once was smart enough not to start that conversation in front of a clerk. A horn tooted outside. "That bastard," she said cheerfully, digging out her cash. She always had cash.

"He's on a mission."

"Is that your nice way of saying he's cruising for a bruising?" She looked at me and laughed. "Never mind, it's okay." The truck honked again. "He's gotta know that'd have the opposite effect on me, right?"

"Morgan let's just go."

"Fine, fine, I bow to your judgment."

# Chapter Seven

L uke didn't say anything at first, just got back on the road and started driving. Finally Joe asked, "What did Grandpa say?"

"He thinks Morgan's idea is a stroke of genius, if you can imagine such a thing."

"I can," she said, grinning.

"When the time comes, we'll meet up with somebody to get a tracker and make sure it works, that song and dance."

"I hope it's Everett," Morgan said. "He's my favorite. You can tell him that."

"You just like him because he likes your ridiculous music," Luke said, feeling for his coffee in the cup holder.

"Got it in one. How'd you Ward boys get so damn smart?" She leaned back and rustled with the newspapers. "Why'd you get three, Allie?"

"Because if I only got one, you would've said why'd you get one."

"Yeah, okay, fair."

"What are you fucking around with behind me?" Luke asked.

"The latest reaches of my fame, of course. I want to see what my bandmates say about me. Oh, they talked to Vinnie, this'll be good." She scanned the pages. I didn't know how she had the light to read, and then I remembered that we could actually pretty much see in the dark. She was quiet for long enough that Luke took a breath to say something else and she said "Vinnie's the drummer, he's a solid guy. He's got a great quote here, it really captures my energy, I feel." She theatrically cleared her throat "'You don't understand, when you ask me where Morgan is, I wouldn't have known where Morgan was anyway. You can text her practically anytime and get an answer, that isn't a problem, but otherwise she disappears for months, a year, and when she comes back, she's at your door at three in the morning with cigarettes and a bottle of Jack and wanting to know if we know anybody with one of those electric guitars that came out of the Soviet Union that have their own effects built in, and she's written the whole next album on like, the backs of receipts and napkins and diner placemats and shit. Once, *one* time, she had a notebook, a really nice leather bound deal with a green ribbon bookmark in it, but you can't expect that of Morgan. You can't expect anything of Morgan. This is Morgan's show, and we're just along for the ride.'" She looked up. "Hunter gave me that notebook for Christmas that year."

"Very thoughtful of her," I said, because she seemed to want an answer.

"What do you get the person who has everything, right?"

"What did you get her?"

"Oh I don't remember. A leather jacket from a consignment shop? Maybe? She wanted something to put pins on."

"Nice of your band mate to cover for you," Joe said after a minute, and she laughed.

"No that...that wasn't covering for me."

"...Oh."

"I wonder if that notebook is in my bag, I think it is. I could probably auction it."

"Why would you have a used up notebook in your bag?" Luke asked.

"Because I'm very sentimental," she said, looking at the paper again, but she didn't read us any more.

"Is Vinnie—" I started to ask.

"No, you didn't meet Vinnie," she said. "You met Al. He's bass. And fake IDs."

Luke huffed a breath out his nose. "Your band lineup aside, what did your manager say? You called your manager?"

"Oh well first he said 'Morgan it's been nine months, what the fuck.' and I told him that I went to the Himalayas for a retreat. Then I told him that reports of my disappearance were grossly exaggerated and I wanted to go on NPR's tinydesk and he said that NPR had too much of a lead time but maybe in another seven months but probably not until the year after next unless the new album was ready and I said that it was getting there and that really woke him up." She lit a cigarette, opening her window halfway.

"So what then?"

"Well he's going to call around and see if anybody wants to have me on for an interview and a three song set, you know how they do it. And then there'll be a party or parties, there always are, blah blah blah." She stopped again, blew smoke out the window, and nobody said anything. "The wheels are in motion, in other words. No solid dates or anything right now. But we should keep ourselves within a certain radius of New York."

"New York is kind of a big—"

"City. The city." She laughed to herself and said "New York City!" in a weird fake accent.

"So we just kind of assume that's on the back burner and keep on with our original plan?"

"Yeah, exactly. It...how to translate it for you." She dragged on her cigarette, winked at me. "It isn't an action item until it is."

"Okay then." Luke kept driving and I wanted to ask what we were doing next, if we were stopping or if we had another mission, but I didn't want to ask. I didn't want Morgan and Luke to start fighting again, and Morgan was on that knife-edge right now and probably would be for a while. Well, when wasn't she?

It was getting light out when Morgan shook me awake. I didn't even realize I'd fallen asleep; I must have just spent the whole night dreaming that we were riding in the back seat of the truck through the night. "I drank your coffee," she said.

"That's okay." I rubbed my eyes. I felt numb and dazed. "Where are we?" She stood outside my open truck door, smoking. The driver's door was also open, keys in the ignition.

"Location two, but the Wards took point this time."

"I'm shocked you let them do such a thing."

"Yeah they were too. Luke almost wouldn't do it. He probably figured I'd just fuckin' drive off or something."

"You would never, with such encouragement to break things." I stretched cautiously.

"Well I know that, and you know that."

"So then why'd he go anyway?"

She shrugged, flicking away her cigarette butt. "I guess he's supposed to make sure Joe sees action."

"Poor Joe." I wondered if Joe's dad gave that directive somehow. Or if it was from Bill. It was more probably from Bill.

"I guess? What do you mean, poor Joe?" She seemed genuinely confused.

"Well for one, he isn't doing the military thing, so I don't know what the point of him 'seeing action' would be, really. Other than if we think this is going to go on for the rest of our lives. Which, I guess if it goes badly, it will be." Morgan blinked at me, surprised this time. "For two, Luke isn't exactly who I'd want guiding and teaching me through this kind of experience."

"Luke's one of the best killers they got, I think," she said. "Anyway, you don't get to choose that kind of thing. As we found out. You wouldn't have chosen me either."

"I didn't choose any of this."

"My point." She shut my door, walked around to the driver's seat. She got in and started the truck, and a second later, Luke and Joe jogged up the road and got in.

"None of it's ours," Luke said without preamble, and Morgan shrugged.

"Whatever. It's your truck."

I started to ask what they were talking about, and then smelled the blood. I looked at Joe, who was blinking a lot. Stunned wasn't really the right word for how he looked, but it was close. "Are you—"

"He's fine." Luke lit a cigarette. "We'll drive about an hour and then there's a campground where we can park. You want me to switch out?"

"I'm okay driving," Morgan said.

Joe turned his head towards me and I knew he wasn't going to say anything, he wasn't going to contradict Luke, but I wasn't sure how okay he was either. We weren't like Luke and Morgan. Oh I hate this, I thought. I *did* make my choice, so that Mama and the boys wouldn't be science experiments, and that was the right thing to do, I believed that firmly. And we had to make Silvernail stop, we just had to. But I didn't really grasp what that ultimately meant, I didn't think, and I hated this.

I put my hand on the seat between us, palm up, and after a second, Joe moved his hand a little to cover mine. My fingers were cold, but I didn't realize it until I felt how warm his were. We sat there like that for most of the hour to the campground, and I just hoped Luke or Morgan wouldn't say anything. I knew for a fact that Morgan at least wasn't really in the comforting business. I didn't know how comforting I was being. I didn't know what happened, and he wasn't going to be able to tell me. He fell asleep, or was pretending to be asleep, before we got there, and I gently took my hand back before anybody noticed.

At the campground, Morgan and Luke went off to the showers, and I looked at my phone like I expected anybody to text me. I just really hoped that Rachel would have, actually. Or maybe Sidney. But no, there wasn't anything. Of course there wasn't. I got out and walked around the truck, stretching my legs, experimentally stretching my good shoulder, and then my hurt one. It felt better, a lot better, and that was dangerous because it meant I'd feel like I could push it. Maybe I didn't need the sling anymore. I laughed a little, quietly. Maybe I was like Morgan, just a little bit. Not in the right ways, of course.

Joe kind of sniffed and started as I got back in the car. "Sorry, I didn't mean to wake you."

"No, it's okay, I should go take a shower." He yawned. He wasn't the one who smelled like blood.

"They'll probably be back soon." I somehow wasn't surprised that we were just going to sleep in the truck. Morgan and I had just slept in the Jeep a few times.

"I'll wait, so you're not alone."

"Thanks." I didn't know if I should laugh or cry, at how thoughtful that was, and it was such a small thing. Everything was just so stressful right now, everything seemed big. "I admit, I'm kind of hesitant about the rock star plan, but if it cuts down on nights like we just had, maybe it'll be fine."

"Yeah, I agree."

"Maybe I'm a little bit selfish, thinking that." I was struck by sudden guilt. We knew what Silvernail did to the people they had, we knew what kind of shape Sela and Rachel were in when we rescued them.

"Stop it, no." He was going to say more, but we heard Luke and Morgan coming back, Morgan laughing, Luke grumbling. "It isn't selfish to be glad of something that you can't stop her from doing anyway."

"I guess not. Sometimes you just gotta lean in."

"Allie, are you hungry?" Morgan yelled when they were in sight.

"Not really."

"Damn it."

"We're going to sleep, and then we'll get something to eat," Luke said, like maybe he'd already said it at least once. He did look tired. And I knew Morgan was tired, but I also knew how long and hard she could and would push through that.

"It's going to be too hot to sleep," Morgan said.

"Not for me."

"Ah yes, all of your military experience," she said, in a tone of voice that said if she couldn't sleep, nobody was going to sleep.

"Yes, exactly. So give it a rest. Literally."

"What if we told Allie where to go and slept while she drove with the AC on? Best of both worlds, we still make time, and don't suffocate."

Luke didn't even look at me. "Allie doesn't want to drive us."

"No, but she would if we asked nice enough."

"I'm right here," I said, laughing a little. Like Morgan ever asked me for anything nice enough.

"Yes, which is important if you're going to drive us." Morgan pulled the towel off of her hair and started to finger comb it. "What happened to those combs we bought?"

"Mine is in my bag." She looked at me, and I went and rummaged in my bag until I found a wide toothed comb to hand her.

"Okay, I'm going to go take a shower," Joe said, when it seemed like we weren't going to drive off that second, and Luke waved him along.

"There isn't any point in pushing ourselves to exhaustion," Luke said. "Exciting as it might seem."

"This isn't my first rodeo," Morgan said.

"No, now it's your second."

"Look, I appreciate your impulse to be...protective of me or whatever, but that just isn't going to work out." She made a face when she got stuck on a knot.

Luke paused in the act of lighting a cigarette. "Is that what you think I'm doing?" He kind of glanced at me.

She grinned. "Is it not?"

"No."

"If you say so." She finished combing her hair, yawned. "Well I'm gonna crawl into the back and sleep until Joe's done anyway. And then we can decide."

"There isn't anything to decide," Luke said, but she was already getting in the back seat, though she left both doors hanging open. He sighed and looked at me. "Do you want one?" He offered me the cigarettes.

"No, thank you. I quit."

He laughed, and I was glad. "Well that's good. It's a bad habit."

"Smelly one too."

He shrugged. "You get used to it."

"I guess." Maybe Morgan, and Luke, and even Rachel smoked to keep from smelling *so much* just all the time. It helped dull things and help the world be a little more approachable. Bill too, with his cigars. But now what was I supposed to talk to Luke Ward about, and for how long? There was only so fast I could expect Joe to be. Morgan was probably already asleep, though she'd be alert at the slightest provocation.

I thought maybe he didn't know what to talk to me about either. Or, he didn't care. Leaned against the front bumper of the truck, he smoked and kind of looked off at the campground, and I sat at the picnic table that was right there and read the newspaper article about Morgan and Howling. The writer of the article suggested using the hashtag #WheresMorgan and I guessed that was why the drummer was so bemused. He also called her a cryptid in a different part of the interview, and while still funny, that was a little close to home.

"Let me see that," Luke said, and I passed it to him. Maybe he was curious about what he'd gotten himself into, but really, I felt like the article only confirmed that Morgan was always herself. He laughed a few minutes later, folding the paper. "Jesus."

"Morgan's Morgan," I said, as though I'd known her for my whole life, not just twenty four hours longer than him.

"Sure fucking seems like it."

"I can hear you," she said from the truck, but in sort of a distant tone.

"Of course you can," I said. "You can hear the person at the check in station by the road too."

"It's my curse."

"We've all got it," I said, maybe a little impatiently. "You're not special."

She barked a surprised laugh. "Shit, Allie."

"Well it's true."

"No, you're right. It's great." She sat up and scooted to the end of the bench seat, dangling her legs out and blinking at us. "Actually it's nice to not have to worry about that right now, on top of everything else. Just spending time with wolves. It's one reason being a rock star works out so great, people expect you to be a little unhinged."

"Did Morgan just say she likes spending time with us?" Joe asked, clearly shocked. He looked more awake, but only marginally. I didn't even hear him coming back, he was just *there*.

"She might've," Luke said. "Miracles do happen."

"So are we gonna go eat now?" She grinned hopefully.

"Fuck it," Luke said. "Might as well."

# Chapter Eight

Luke got a call from Bill towards the end of breakfast and went outside with it. Our next assignment, maybe. I shuddered a little, and both Joe and Morgan looked at me.

"I'm not great at this," I admitted.

"That's gonna be too bad when you have to go in one of these times," Morgan said.

"I'll handle it." I handled it when we went in to get Rachel, I didn't say.

"Maybe you won't have to," Joe said.

"I'm not holding my breath." I still wasn't wearing my sling, and had been able to handle breakfast so far, anyway. The bullet wound still twinged sometimes but my collarbone finally felt more bruised than broken. Which probably wasn't true but maybe it was.

"You've done pretty okay in crisis, Allie, it's when you think about it that you get all hung up. Just don't think about it." Morgan dropped her napkin on the table.

"Thanks for the advice."

"I do what I can." She finished her coffee, looking at her phone. It occurred to me that Rachel had probably been in contact with Ardith. Whether Ardith then told Hunter, or what she said about it to Morgan, was the question. Probably nothing. I was probably just hoping for connections that weren't there. I was just hoping that after all of this, Rachel didn't mean it, and we would have a home to go to with the aunts. But Rachel didn't say things she didn't mean. I knew that, Morgan definitely knew that. I wondered how much she even thought about it, as I watched her text back. I always assumed it was Hunter.

Luke came back and sat down. "They're keeping it out of the news where they can, anyway," he said. "The warehouse was a fire call of course, but they called it a gas leak and blamed the propane and a pilot light or something."

"I don't know if that's good or bad," I said.

"It means their rules of engagement seem to be the same. They want to handle this all on their own, and get test subjects out of it."

"Do we still have the network back doors?" Joe asked.

"Yes, but they're trying to use it sparingly, so they don't lose it, while trying to make more connections." Luke looked at his plate like he didn't remember finishing everything, then looked at his watch. "Alright, we should get going. Everybody go to the bathroom so we're not stopping a million times."

"Sure thing, Pops," Morgan said, I assume just to see what his face did. She was disappointed, though; he must've been expecting something, if not exactly that, because his face didn't change at all.

He stood up and dropped cash on the table. "See you outside."

"I think we've really grown on him," she said, laughing.

"He's going to leave you on the side of the road one of these times," I said.

"He won't, but I'd understand the impulse."

"I wouldn't be so sure," Joe said, shaking his head.

"Well how about we bet on it? Nothing big, just a dollar?"

"You want me to bet you that Luke will leave you by the side of the road?"

"That's what I said. If he does, I owe you a dollar. If he doesn't, you owe me a dollar. See, nice low stakes."

I said, "I think the stakes are a little more complicated than—" and Morgan held up her hand.

"Shake on it, Joe?"

"Sure," he said, laughing. "Nice low stakes." They shook hands.

"See, I know Joe won't do anything to ensure that I'll get left by the side of the road, he's terminally honest. Everett, I couldn't make this kind of bet with."

"I thought you said Everett was your favorite."

"He's my favorite techie, anyway."

"Do you even remember anybody else's name?" I asked.

"Techies, no. Medics, yes."

"I should've expected that, I know your priorities."

"My priorities are either keeping my blood inside or being friendly with the people who can do that, which is perfectly reasonable."

"You don't act like you want to keep your blood inside," Joe said, before I could.

"Neither do you, if you keep making comments like that," Morgan said, smiling sweetly as she got up.

We each took our turns in the single-occupancy restrooms and got back to the truck, where Luke had a map open against the steering wheel. He passed it to Joe when he got in. "Fold that, would you?"

"What's our next assignment?" Morgan asked.

"Other than Elvis Has Left the Building?"

"Shut up, it is not called that."

He laughed. "No, it isn't."

"He's making jokes all on his own now, should we be worried?" Morgan said in a fake whisper, leaned over to me and to Joe.

"Probably," Joe said, folding the map. "It probably means the real fun is about to start."

"The *real* fun? Luke, you've been holding out on me?"

He grinned at her in the rear view and no, I didn't like that look at all. "We had to get more acquainted, you understand."

Clearly, Morgan liked that look. "Of course, of course. So what's the fun?"

"Okay, so most corporate places just have their servers managed by a company at server farms. New York City, out in the Arizona desert, someplace in Europe, whatever right?"

"Right?"

"Well, these guys don't do that. Or, not with all their servers. I guess their ones not to do with kidnapping and illegal experiments are fine in a normal server farm, but otherwise they've got a server or servers that we'd be very interested in, off the Jersey Turnpike in another one of those places that's too much lawn and just a little building, that they seem to like."

"It'll be hard to set Allie up with a rifle, in a place like that," Morgan said, glancing at me.

"Sure would. So we're all going in on this one. After hours, to minimize personnel involvement."

"But not..." I trailed off, looking away and down.

"No, not empty, they have security. What do you want me to say, that there's just one old guy who sits in a guard shack and who's three days from retirement so he's not gonna take any risks?" I didn't say anything. "These people are more than happy to hurt you. You're not doing yourself any favors if you're unwilling to hurt them." I expected him to keep going, keep digging in the way Mama would if she was reprimanding me. He didn't, and I looked up, surprised. He seemed to be thinking something over, and we all waited him out, even Morgan. "It's better when people like me, or Morgan, can go in. But we don't always have that luxury."

"I know," I said.

"Now can we get on with it?" Morgan asked.

"As always, the simplest plan is the best plan. We get in, we grab servers, we get out. After, we drive to meet techs, including your favorite Everett, to get the tracker and troubleshoot it and get some shuteye."

"Are we going to sleep *before* the, uh, mission too?" I asked.

"Yes, Pollyanna, we're going to sleep before the mission too." Luke laughed. "You'll recall I already tried to steer us towards that and somebody kept pushing."

"And then we had a nice breakfast and can find an advantageous place to crash now," Morgan said.

"The campground was fine."

"Then why'd we leave?"

Luke flexed his hands on the steering wheel. "Because there's more to leadership than being right."

"*Leadership*," Morgan crowed.

"Gotta set a good example for the kids. Joe don't say anything, I remember you in diapers."

"Now who's sentimental," Morgan said, lighting a cigarette.

"That's not what I mean." She dragged on the cigarette and waited. Definitely me and Joe weren't going to say anything. "When you see a kid grow up, they're always a kid to you, right? Or like when we got somebody new in the unit, they were always the new guy, even when they weren't anymore."

"I get it," Morgan said, laughing just a little. "You softie."

In some ways, I thought, it was good that she kept needling him like this. Figuring out where the boundaries and soft spots were when we were someplace comparatively safe. But I didn't know if that was the kind of logic Morgan was actually following, or if she was just going to act like this regardless. Probably act like this regardless, but also she'd had elements of a plan steps ahead of where we were, like when she bought the carabiners and spray paint before we rescued Rachel, and when she got the handcuffs right before we had a further Silvernail plan involving the Wards.

We finally stopped again at one of the Ward camps in Pennsylvania. Nobody else was there, but it had little cabins, and we each had privacy and slept until evening. When Morgan knocked on my door to wake me up in the gloaming, she was practically zinging with energy, and I both knew enough to be wary and also that there was nothing I could do about it.

"Just a couple of highway hours to the place," she said. "Then in and out, easy peasy."

"Easy peasy," I repeated. Nothing was easy peasy, not ever. And not with Morgan.

Luke's mood seemed to have improved some, anyway, and I made a mental note that lack of sleep apparently made him even more stern and grumpy than we normally knew him to be. Joe gave me an uncertain look and I shrugged; we were doing this, whether we were really ready to be or not. I thought of his wide eyes when he got back in the truck this morning. The smell of blood. Easy peasy, right.

I even dozed off again in the truck, as Joe and Morgan amicably squabbled over the radio. I didn't recall hearing Luke ever actually mention a music preference once; he'd asked her to play Freebird, but that was just something you did when somebody had a guitar.

We parked in what was labeled a commuter lot, and while still in the truck, passed around the hoodies and masks to cover our heads and faces. We got out of the truck and walked into the woods, and we'd been walking for a few minutes before I realized Morgan was carrying a shotgun, and of course Luke had his handgun, but me and Joe didn't have anything. Well, I had a jackknife and probably Joe did too, but I didn't know that anybody was counting that.

"Morgan, what about—" I stopped myself. What was I going to ask, why didn't I have a way to hurt somebody? I didn't want to hurt anybody, that was my answer.

"You and Joe will be our pack mules," she said. "That okay?"

"More than okay," I said. I didn't know when they decided that, maybe when I was asleep.

Luke hushed us and Morgan stuck out her tongue, and we kept walking. Then we stopped and we all put the masks on and pulled our hoods up, and they smelled like laundry detergent and drying on the line. I imagined Bill Ward's wife doing the wash like this for her boys, humming as she took the hamper outside, and it was funny but not, a laugh catching sideways in my throat.

They didn't even have a fence on the wooded side of things. They probably expected, with good reason, that nobody in that commuter lot would ever even look in this direction, much less breach the treeline and walk for like ten minutes to get here. And then if they did, what would they find? A wide green lawn, a little square one-story building with its own parking lot for maybe ten cars. No signs. There was just one car in the lot, the night security obviously. Or maybe a janitor. Maybe it would be their break time, and they'd be eating dinner outside someplace. But I didn't smell anybody outside. I did smell deer, three or four of them, moving away from us, quietly but deliberately.

There was a keypad at the door but also a regular lock on the door itself, and Luke fiddled with it for a few minutes while Morgan watched the parking lot, holding the shotgun casually but ready, things in the mechanism clicking, and clicking, and then the clunk when the door unlocked. He hooked a carabiner in the lock plate, and I had a second to wonder if it was one of Morgan's and then I bit my lip so I could focus. We went inside quietly, single file, through a foyer with a coat closet, to a T hallway that led off dimly in both directions. I was glad that it wasn't just full of buzzing fluorescent lights. The center of the building was made up of glass partitions, some of them clear glass, some of them frosted, and the floor hummed with all of the electricity and computer fans.

Morgan went left immediately and Joe followed and I hesitated but ended up going right with Luke. Looking for a door into the server area. How big was a server, anyway? I thought they sounded like big huge things, and I knew we were strong, and Luke had a truck, but—

When it happened, it happened quickly. The security guard maybe heard the door, maybe saw us on a camera, I didn't know, but he came at Luke fast and strong from behind one of the central panes of frosted glass, in the intermittently lit hallway. He had a gun on his belt, unsnapped, and he had something that he hit Luke with, and Luke's gun slid across the floor and fetched up against the wall. Luke gave a surprised grunt as they kind of wrestled close in, and his head snapped back and I could smell blood and then he did something that made the guard cry out and fall back a step. That would bring Morgan, I thought, frozen in place. Morgan would come fix this, if Luke didn't.

But Luke faltered, and didn't close in with the guard again right away, shaking his head, and I couldn't see what was wrong with him, but I could see that the guard was reaching back on his belt for his gun and Morgan wasn't going to get here in any kind of time unless she started smashing through all that glass and I heard her running but there wasn't enough time and I didn't let myself think, I ran and I slid on my knees on the linoleum to Luke's gun, picked up Luke's gun and fumbled for a second at the safety and its click was the loudest thing in the world at that moment, until I sucked in a quick breath and swung around, coming up on one knee, breathing out and pulling the trigger all at once when I thought the guard was in my sights. Then the gun was the loudest thing in the world, and the whine in my ears that followed, and Luke was arming blood off the eyeholes of his mask and Morgan was dragging me to my feet, and I was pointing the gun away from her, away from Luke, at the floor. I couldn't think of where the safety was to put it back on. Where was Joe? The guard was on the floor. The guard was on the floor and there was starting to be a lot of blood on the floor and Luke reached down and pulled the gun off his belt, shoved it in the back of his jeans, and turned to me and Morgan. I watched his posture change a little as he cocked his head, looking at her hands, and then looked at mine.

"Joe's unplugging the server stuff. I told him to stay put," Morgan said to him, her voice distant. Had she been talking to me and I couldn't hear her?

"Okay, good." His voice sounded thick, off. With the masks, I still couldn't tell what happened. He came and took the gun from me, surprisingly gentle. I was glad he took it. It was heavy, and I didn't know if I could put it down on my own. My hands started to shake once I wasn't holding it anymore. He engaged the safety, holstered it, gave me an assessing look. "Let's go get that shit pulled. We need to be out of here ASAP."

"Is he...did I..." Of course he was. Of course I did. What else did I think was going to happen? I was breathing hard, but we were all breathing hard, it was hot anyway, and we were in hoodies and masks besides, and we went back the way Morgan came. Joe had one thing unplugged and pulled loose in its rack and was working on another. He barely looked up when we came through the door, just pointed at another rack.

"The top one there, Everett said. Assuming their labeling is right." The whine was fading from my hearing, but Joe still sounded underwater.

"If it isn't right, I'm personally coming back here to burn this fucker down. Which maybe is what we should've done," Luke growled, giving the equipment a yank. "Morgan, get the wires." She did, and without comment, and Joe looked at them, and then looked at me and shrugged. "Is that it?"

"That we know of," Joe said. He doesn't know, I thought. He just knew he heard a gunshot and Luke smelled like blood and both of those things went together like normal.

"Let's move out."

I started to pick up one of the server boxes and Morgan got it instead, and Joe had the first one, so I was empty handed as we walked out. I pulled off the carabiner so the door would close and lock behind us. Looking across the lawn, the deer I smelled earlier were grazing there, tails flicking, heads coming up occasionally to look around.

We were almost to the truck before my knees gave out. I'd been trying to do the Morgan thing, just compartmentalize, just concentrate on what we were doing, eyes forward on the next thing, but what we were doing was walking calmly through woods, carrying computer stuff, after I killed somebody, and it crashed down on me just like that. Morgan said something to Luke, who crouched down a little so she could put her server box on top of the one he was carrying, and she came to get me. Joe hesitated and Luke said his name sharply, and they kept walking, Joe looking back once.

We all still had our masks on, and it wasn't until Morgan pulled mine off that I felt like I was allowed to panic breathe, in big whooping, wheezing gasps that surprised me with their force. "Allie, we gotta get to the truck," she said. I looked at her, wide-eyed; she had that look on her face that was caught partway between impatience and regret.

"I killed—" My throat closed on my words and for a second I just couldn't breathe at all, and she shook me, hard, until I gasped again.

"Yeah, and if you didn't, he would've killed Luke, and then we would've been worse off than we already are. Who else is gonna drive around with us like this? You want to do ops with Joe's grandpa? You did what you had to do, you did it fast and clean and good. We survived. And now we need to go. I wish you had more time to freak out here but you don't, we have to go, and if you won't get up, I will carry you and it will be embarrassing. You can freak out in the truck."

I did good. I killed somebody good. I didn't think I could get up, but Morgan stood up and stood me up with her. "I never wanted to. Do that." Was I making sense? She took my arm, started pulling me along.

"I know." For just a second, she looked just like Rachel, telling us to never come back.

# Chapter Nine

Morgan told me I could freak out in the truck but I didn't know how, once we were there. I fastened my seatbelt and folded my hands in my lap but they wouldn't stay clasped together nicely, falling apart and instead just crouching and quivering next to each other like rabbits. Which made me think of the rabbits we took out of the cages, the night we rescued Rachel. What happened to those rabbits, I wondered. Did they get outside? Did they get burned up in the fire?

I shuddered and then I kept shuddering and I felt lightheaded all the sudden so I put my head on my knees. Was that what you were supposed to do? Morgan sighed and put her hand on my back and I wanted to shrug her off, hard, but lacked the courage to do it. We kept being in situations where Morgan was the only one to comfort me, but also Morgan was the least suited person to comfort anybody. I didn't think anybody had comforted me in my life, and I didn't know what I wanted from it either, so maybe it wasn't fair, being mad at Morgan for it. Just like it wasn't fair being mad at Morgan for not coming to us quicker. For not killing that man before I had to, because Morgan didn't seem to be bothered by killing people. Or Luke.

"Is she okay?" Luke asked after awhile or maybe not much time at all. Why was he asking? To see if they needed to leave me with whatever Wards we were meeting?

"It's been five fucking minutes, she just needs some time," Morgan snapped. "You should know that." She was impatient with me but she'd still defend me.

He audibly bit off the next thing he was going to say. "I meant, does she need anything," he said after a pause, in a clearly measured tone.

Morgan made kind of a noncommittal noise and I sat up, suddenly furious at him, lightheaded and still trembling. "Why do you care?" I asked, not yelling but definitely too loud. "You didn't care about Joe this morning. Why would you care about me? Especially if I'm such a *liability*?"

Morgan laughed in the sudden stunned silence. "Can't say shit like that around Allie right when she's gone to sleep. She latches on somehow."

"Apparently." He looked over his shoulder at me, and I finally saw his face. His nose was swollen, maybe broken, and he had a nasty cut over his left eyebrow. "I care because you saved my life. Is that good enough?"

"Yes," I said, because it made sense and because I wanted him to look at the road again.

"Okay then. Thank you." Luke straightened out again. "Should I ask everybody, is that what you want? Yeah? Is everybody okay? Does anybody need anything?" His tone wasn't the nicest, but he also wasn't being mean, not really.

Morgan's phone rang, and I looked at her. She looked at the phone, then rolled her eyes and answered it. "Talk to me, Neil. Okay, good. Yes. When? No, Saturday's fine, it's good." She paused a second, maybe trying to remember what day it was.

"Wednesday," Joe said quietly and she nodded.

"You already talked to everybody else? Cool, good. Yeah, text me the studio address. Yeah, I'll send a set list. Three songs? No, tell them four. Yes, I'm sure you do have ideas about it. See you Saturday." She hung up while Neil was still talking, but he was probably used to that by now. I watched her type up and send a long text. "Yes, Neil is the band's manager, yes that's this Saturday, remember I said that it maybe would be a wait and then something fast. I just sent Hunter a shopping list, her and Allie and I will get a hotel room after we touch base with your techs, and I'll make my rock star transformation."

"Your...transformation," Luke repeated.

"You'll just have to watch the livestream," she said, grinning. "Let's stop for milkshakes, that'll be nice, right? Everybody likes milkshakes. You want a milkshake Allie?"

"Okay," I said. My stomach felt like jelly, so maybe it was an awful idea, or maybe it would help. Maybe sugar would help. I've just had a shock, I thought. At least I didn't throw up.

"Milkshakes, okay," Luke said, like Morgan was just playing another joke. "McDonald's okay or do you have something fancier in mind that's on the way?"

"Fancier would be nice but also McDonald's will take less time. There's places down the Shore I love, but not right now. And anyway, some places just get out of control, it's like when they have a rotisserie chicken in your Bloody Mary. Milkshakes don't need all that shit."

Luke took that in for a second. "McDonald's it is then." I watched my hands shake some more. It was so quiet in the truck, and I didn't think it was just because of my ears.

• • • •

THE MILKSHAKE DIDN'T fix anything, but I did feel steadier by the time we went through a drive thru and got two vanilla milkshakes and one strawberry for Joe. Luke got coffee, even with Morgan goading him quietly enough that the person taking the orders wouldn't pick it up. Not even a fancy coffee, just black coffee.

"You and Rachel, with your black coffee," she said, and then I saw a look cross her face that was a mixture of surprise and hurt. It was almost funny, that her carelessness could hurt even herself. Instead of laughing, though, tears sprang to my eyes, and I got my straw in on the second try and drank my milkshake. I wondered if she even had the capacity to be worried about this plan of hers, or if she was just fully committed to the whole spirit of it. Having a live performance. Getting caught on purpose. Leading the Wards to yet another secret lab. Hopefully bringing it all crashing down the final time. How many secret labs could Silvernail possibly be willing to sacrifice for this? Or maybe Morgan was counting on them having lost their remote labs, and this one would be the real deal, where most of the legitimate work got done, and it would be at tremendous risk bringing her there. Maybe she explained that all already and I missed it, because what I thought wasn't important enough.

"I don't suppose I could get you to swing through a liquor store," Morgan said.

"You're right, you can't," Luke said.

"Like, ever, or just right now?" She was grinning but she was irritated.

"Just right now."

"What if I said it was medicinal? For Allie." I flinched and looked at her and she winked. She didn't know Mama put brandy in my coffee that night. I never told her, or anybody. No. I told the aunts.

"I'd know you were lying," Luke said, even as I heard Joe take a breath to say something. "I get it, I understand the impulse, but we're operating sober right now."

"And I think *you're* lying, but I guess that's fine." She sent another text.

"Adding it to your shopping list?" I asked, trying for sarcasm.

Her phone buzzed. "Yeah, Hunter has me covered."

"Speaking of Hunter," Luke said, and Morgan shot me another glance that I had no way to read in my current state, or maybe ever. "Any word on your new vehicle?"

She laughed. "What, are you really that eager to get rid of me? I don't blame you." Luke heaved a sigh.

"I just expected you to be crawling out of your skin by now, having to drive around with us."

"I *do* have self control," Morgan said with elaborate stiffness. I laughed, but the edge of it had a wobble that scared me, and Joe turned on the radio.

• • • •

LIKE EVERY OTHER ARRIVAL at a Ward location, Luke and Morgan were called inside by Bill and me and Joe were left to our own devices. The techs got the servers out of the back of the truck, and one of them cast an inquisitive glance at Morgan's music equipment before he saw me looking and went off with the others.

"Are you hungry?" Joe asked.

"Just tired," I said. It was so late at night that it was early in the morning. "Do you think it would be okay if I crashed somewhere?"

"Yeah, let's find you a room." It was a two story house off of kind of a quiet local road, with a long driveway and in a little scrap of woods. They didn't have dogs here. It sounded like the war room was either in the basement, or a room off the back of the house, and as I followed Joe upstairs, I could hear Morgan's hard-edged laugh. The one she did where nobody else in the room was laughing, and she was daring them to stop her. I stopped, my hand gripping the bannister; I felt like I should go to her. Back her up. "Come on," Joe said quietly.

"I just thought..." I trailed off. She would be fine. It was her plan, they had to make sure it was solid. They didn't need me for that.

"I know, it's okay." It was all bedrooms up here, not all of them empty, but Joe found me an empty one, with a full bed and a trunk at the foot of it with pillows and folded blankets on top. I sat on the bed, slowly untied my boots and pulled them off, while he kind of hovered in the doorway. He didn't know what to do, and I didn't either.

"I don't want to be alone," I said finally, almost ashamed of myself. "I shouldn't ask you for anything but I don't want to be alone."

"I can stay," he said, and he hesitated. "Luke told me what happened. You don't need to say anything about it."

"Thank you." I pushed the sheets back and they smelled like the same detergent that the masks did and I had a moment where I wondered if I was going to be able to take my next breath, but I only had a little hitch. We both kind of waited awkwardly.

"Just lay down," he said after a second. "It's okay. I'll sit with you."

"You could sleep too, if you wanted," I said, a little shyly. I just had too much noise in my head to make sense of all the feelings that I had, that we both had, that were snarled together. What I was thinking of was when my little brothers had bad dreams and they came to me in the night. About how I could never do that, never go to Mama in the night. She never let me in. "That would be okay."

"If you're sure," he said.

"I'm sure," I said, a little more firmly. I got into the bed and moved over enough that I thought he'd have room. He took one of the extra pillows from the top of the trunk and put it next to mine, sat on the edge of the bed to take his boots off.

Since I got shot, I'd been sleeping on my back, but that just felt too exposed right now, and I curled up on my left side. Joe laid on his back at first, and I was pretty sure that we were both just laying there in the dark listening to each other breathe. That was the problem with senses like ours, we could hear bits and scraps of noise from the whole house. The deep rumble of Bill's voice. Morgan laughing. A door banging as somebody went outside to smoke a cigarette. It must be nice, to have that built in excuse. I'm going outside to smoke. I was such a goody goody I'd only ever tried a cigarette the once, and it very much didn't agree with me. Nobody would ever believe me, if I pretended to take up smoking to have that escape hatch. Not even being around all of Morgan's smoking made me smell authentically enough. Not to wolves.

Eventually, hesitantly, carefully, Joe also rolled over on his left side, and put his arm over me. That was what I'd wanted, but didn't know how to ask for. Didn't let myself ask for. But finally, finally, I felt the shock and tension running out of my muscles, and I relaxed slowly, our breathing slowly matching up, and then slipped off to sleep feeling safe.

# Chapter Ten

When I woke up, I was alone again, but Joe's side of the bed was still warm. That was okay, it wasn't like he snuck off in the night. Maybe his leaving was why I woke up. I listened, and thought maybe I heard him on the stairs. I thought he was still carrying his boots. The room was golden with sunshine, and the house smelled like coffee, the way all wolf houses seemed to in the morning. I wondered how it happened that way, or maybe it couldn't be all wolf houses. Just Culvers and Wards, and if we went to the Coutard's they'd do something else. But, like how I thought Rachel and Morgan and Luke all smoked for a reason, I wondered if coffee was something like that too. That it went well with our makeup somehow, in the way that chocolate absolutely did not. Maybe I would ask Fran, if I ever saw her again. I couldn't imagine asking Morgan and getting anything like a satisfying answer. Or anything other than made fun of, actually.

And there was another surprise, that she didn't come and find me after her meeting with Bill and Luke was up, didn't laugh at the moment of solace that I had. I would've thought it would be too good for her to pass up. Maybe she was just glad to not have to babysit me for once. I rolled onto my back, inhaled the smell of recently sleeping Joe, and closed my eyes again to play a game, whether I could figure out where Morgan was in the house. I could smell that she was here, of course. I couldn't hear her, which probably meant she was sleeping for once. I thought maybe she was downstairs in one of the rooms there, but I also didn't know how many bedrooms this place could possibly have. I didn't exactly get, or ask for, the tour.

I could hear Joe talking to somebody in the kitchen. Not Bill, he was on a lower timbre than everybody else. There were so many Wards here that I didn't know, it wasn't any fun to try to guess. That brought me up short; since when was I expecting to have fun?

I spent some time carefully stretching my shoulder, sore but so much better, then put my boots on and went to find a bathroom and go downstairs. Joe had a cup of coffee poured for me, black, even though Morgan hadn't included me in that taunt yesterday. I put stuff in it sometimes, but mostly I didn't, and I was surprised and touched that he'd noticed. Maybe she hadn't. "Morning," he said.

"Morning," I said. It was Luke in the kitchen with him, and Everett. The band's all back together, I thought, but didn't say. That was a Morgan thing to say. "Did you get the tracker thing figured out already?"

"Yeah, it's good to go," Everett said. "It's on the back of her neck near the hairline, and the glue will last awhile, even with showers or whatever."

I didn't know what 'or whatever' was, maybe whatever energetics Morgan got up to while performing her music. "And what, you have an app or whatever where you can see her on a map?"

"Pretty much." He pulled out his phone, tapped a few things on the screen, and then showed me. "It won't have a map of the inside of the house, of course, but you can tell that she's here and not in motion."

"For once," I said, and Luke gave a short laugh.

"Yeah, when the time comes, we're sending you in to wake her up. It's not safe for the rest of us."

"I'm flattered you think it's safe for me." Or you think I'm expendable, I thought, but they laughed and I laughed with them. "Really, she's gonna sense that we're talking about her and come crashing out of wherever yelling about it." We all stopped, and cocked our heads.

"Maybe not," Joe said, when she didn't manifest.

"Whenever she does finally crash, it's hard. That girl doesn't do anything halfway." Luke finished his coffee and looked at his watch. "And we're on her fucking timetable now. Unless you have a way to reach Hunter?"

"Me? No, I don't." It never occurred to me to ask for Hunter's number. My phone had two numbers saved in it: Morgan and Rachel. A phone ago I had Sidney too, but we almost never kept them for long enough to bother putting more in, and who else was I going to need to call? It wasn't like I had friends. It wasn't like I'd ever really had friends.

"There she is," Bill said, coming into the kitchen. "You just snuck off last night. You sleep okay?"

"I did, thank you." There wasn't any good reason to point out that I didn't do any sneaking, I just wasn't included. Or that I was so tired and upset that talking to me wouldn't have done any good. Was I still upset? Probably, but it felt like it was somewhere else. On a shelf, in a cabinet.

"Good. You kids have been doing great work so far, I just wanted to make sure you heard it from me. I never know what these knuckleheads will pass on." He chuckled a little, and accepted a cup of coffee from Joe.

"Thank you," I said again. This was the best mood I'd ever seen Bill in and just didn't know how to take it. I hoped I didn't look as confused as I felt. Maybe it had just been long enough since one of us broke his truck windshield with a tire iron.

"Hey Luke, you—" Morgan brought herself up short coming through the kitchen door, like she somehow didn't know who-all was in the kitchen. "Oh, it's the whole family."

"I was just telling Allie here that you were doing such good work. And I was just about to tell Allie here that I hope you're careful in the city."

"Oh, Allie's the carefullest," Morgan said, not even looking at me. "Right cuz?"

"Right." Me with Morgan and Hunter. I didn't stand a chance. I drank my coffee.

"Well at least one of you is," Bill said, unbothered. "I forgot last night, do you need cash?"

"Nah, I'm fine. We'll be getting the rock star treatment, remember."

"How could we forget," Luke said. It was interesting to me, maybe a little confusing, how much he didn't like this plan. Maybe he just wasn't involved enough.

"Where are we meeting Hunter?" I asked.

"We've got a hotel room in Newark and then we'll take the train in. So Luke will drop us there a little later."

"We're carrying all that stuff on a train?" I asked.

"There'll be three of us, it's fine. And just the strat and the pedalboard, I can handle that myself even. It's fine, leaving that other stuff with you? I can trust you boys with the acoustics, right?"

"Yes," Luke said impatiently.

"Good, perfect, I knew we could count on you. Everett, you want to check to make sure this chippy thing survived the night?"

He put his coffee down. "Yeah, let me see." She bundled up her hair and turned around and it occurred to me, and I think Everett at the same time, what an intimate place they'd chosen to hide the tracker. "Didn't budge," he said, a little shortly.

"Then we're golden." She grinned at the room. "Why do you all look like that? I thought you'd be more excited for me."

I laughed. I was the only one.

· · · ·

HUNTER WAS STANDING on the sidewalk in front of the hotel waiting for us. She waved cheerfully at Luke, who lifted some of his fingers off the steering wheel as a gesture back. "He really *is* a sourpuss," she said as we made our way inside.

"I told you," Morgan said. "I am an excellent judge of character."

"Well you say that and frankly it's a little suspect."

"Allie, don't you think I'm a good judge of character?" Morgan turned to me in appeal, grinning.

"Oh sure," I said. "You always know exactly how best to piss somebody off."

Hunter laughed so loud that it echoed in the lobby, and a conversation at the check in desk went momentarily quiet. "I'm looking forward to spending more time together, Allie," she said.

"Thanks." I wanted to ask her if she'd talked to Rachel. I assumed Ardith would have. I didn't ask her about Rachel.

We made it up the elevator without incident, and even into the room, Morgan depositing guitar and pedal board cases in the closet with almost more care than I'd seen her use with anything. I looked at the long, low, wide dresser and the items arrayed there. Two big square liquor bottles, a carton of cigarettes, four rolls of tin foil, some assorted tubs and bottles and bowls and things that I assumed were for hair dying. A couple of shopping bags that smelled like clothes. A makeup bag.

"First things first, we need to do your hair," Hunter said. "That's gonna take *forever.*"

"And it'll reek. Do the windows open?" She looked at me, and I went and checked.

"Partway."

"Good enough for government work." Morgan turned the TV on as I got our windows as open as they'd go. She flicked through the channels until she found a music channel and tossed the remote on the bed.

"So what do we—" I started to ask, and Morgan waved her hand.

"You don't need to do anything. Just don't get in my way."

"Morgan stop being mean to your cousin," Hunter said, cracking open the biggest bleach bottle while reading something on her phone.

"I'm not! I just meant she could relax." Morgan looked at me. "Was I being mean?"

"You were being you," I said carefully.

"Shit, now who's being mean."

Hunter shook her head, measuring stuff into the bowl. "It's almost like you're related, it's uncanny."

"Let's livestream some of this, as a teaser."

"You're such a fucking diva." Hunter seemed satisfied with the bowl of stuff she mixed, and Morgan was right, it did reek.

"Look, it would be a damn shame if nobody watched the thing on Saturday because they didn't know about it."

"It sure would. Sit on the bed so I can section your hair. What do you do to protect the underbits?"

"Oh I don't remember, wrap that in tinfoil separately I guess."

"What's the foil for?" I asked.

"Helps the bleach cook," Morgan said. "Do you want to record for us? I lied about you relaxing I guess. Other than that."

"I could do that, yeah. How?"

"Hunter has my instagram phone someplace."

"It's in my purse, over there," Hunter jerked her chin at it. It occurred to me that, other than Mama, I hadn't been around somebody carrying a purse since before I knew I was a wolf.

"A *purse*, I forgot you were a fancy bitch."

"God knows how." By the time I found the phone and got it powered on, Morgan had her shirt off and was in jeans and a sport bra and unlaced boots with a towel around her neck, Hunter folding the under part of her hair that was staying black in hopefully-protective foil. And she wanted me to put her on the internet like that.

"Give me that, I'll get it ready for you to press play." She started typing. "Okay today's Thursday right? The thing is the day after tomorrow?"

"Right." It was both funny but also made sense that Morgan's sense of time was vague at best, with the kind of life she clearly liked leading. I didn't know if I believed her when she told me she never even went to school, I both didn't think that Rachel would've just let that slide and didn't know how Frances was a doctor if they didn't do school.

"Okay, good. This is a smoking room, right?"

"For you?" Hunter asked. "Always."

"Perfect, thanks babe." She opened the carton, unraveled the plastic from one of the packs of cigarettes, and with a cigarette stuck to her bottom lip, slapped her pockets for a lighter, looking around.

"In my purse," Hunter said again, taking the bleach stuff to the bathroom, and I dutifully went and got a plastic lighter from her purse, tossed it to Morgan when she just opened and closed her hand at me.

I followed them into the bathroom. "When should I start it?"

"Hunter, make sure it looks okay."

Hunter looked at the screen, squinted a little, moved my hands to frame Morgan better as she lit her cigarette, and then pressed the go live button. I didn't need to do anything but stand there, but still felt a little rush of adrenaline.

"Apparently some people have been asking where's Morgan," Morgan said, blowing out a cloud of smoke. One of the liquor bottles was on the countertop next to her. "Well fuck you, here's Morgan. Tune in on Saturday morning, details someplace, for a Howling livestream. We'll play a favorite or two, play a surprise, and play a new song. From all the comments I get, it seemed like you assholes wanted to see how I got ready. So step one, my hair gets bleached."

"Why did you hashtag this 'sorry Brad Mondo'?" Hunter asked, starting to put the bleach on.

"Oh, 'cause of the box dye that I used like…six months ago."

"Eight," I said.

"'Cause of the box dye that I used eight months ago," she said, dragging on her cigarette again and grinning at either me or the camera. Grinning at her imagined fans.

"Oh shit. Sorry Brad Mondo," Hunter said, almost giggling. "Maybe you're getting a haircut too."

"Yeah maybe, but not on the livestream. Or at least not for free. Tell your friends, kids. I'll be personally offended if you aren't all there ready and waiting on Saturday." She took a swig from the bottle, cigarette still between two of her fingers, and I wondered if bleach was flammable. "Okay cut."

I pressed the end button, and handed her the phone. She looked at the screen for awhile, took another drink, put the phone on the counter. "Short and sweet," Hunter said.

"You know it." Her regular phone buzzed. "Oh yeah, I should probably tell the band about the new song."

"They just learned about it by watching your livestream, huh?" I asked. My eyes were starting to water from the fumes, and I looked at the switches on the wall until I found the exhaust fan.

"They sure did. It's fine, it's not the first time."

"What would you do if they said they're not playing that song?"

She frowned at me and took another drink. "Solo it? What kind of question is that?"

"Silly me." I went back out into the room, to get away from the bleach, and smoke, and her glare. I heard Hunter say mean again, and Morgan just laughed. I sat on the bed and looked at the tv, but I didn't know what different I would want to watch.

I wasn't equipped to sit around in a hotel room for two days with my rock star cousin and her girlfriend, but it was better than sitting around with the Wards' without her.

I didn't mean to fall asleep. I'd just slept part of the night, after all, but when I woke up, Morgan was towel drying her hair in front of the mirror, the bottle three quarters empty, and Hunter was shining her phone flashlight on it. "Well team, it looks like we maybe actually did it," she said.

"It's not a sorry?" I asked blearily.

"It is not. It needs toning but somehow Hunter got it damn near perfect."

"Hunter reads instructions on things," she said. "And watched the same fail videos that you did? Where does he actually say what people should do right?"

"Like I pay attention to that part." Morgan looked at me in the mirror. "You want a milkshake? We're ordering in."

"Are you ordering food or just milkshakes?" Did I want either? I couldn't tell yet. I stood up and stretched, yawning.

"Food too, I guess, if you want to be like that about it." Her phone buzzed again. "Fucking seriously Al you're just bass it's fine."

"You know he can't hear you," Hunter said, taking the bottle from her.

"I say it out loud so that I text him something more reasonable. Like Vinnie, I fucking tell him a time signature and sing him a melody and he's got the fill of my dreams just ready to go. Al thinks he's Flea or something."

"I have no idea what you just said." Hunter looked at me. "Do you know what she just said?"

"Flea is a famous bassist," I said. "And yes."

"Maybe if Al was a *better* bassist, I'd give him a more complicated bassline..." Morgan lit another cigarette and frowned at her phone.

"Great, I'm surrounded." Hunter took a drink, but jumped and spilled some down her front when her phone rang. "Ardith, hi, what?" She listened for a second. "Oh fuck, sorry, did I use the wrong card? Yeah, no, that's okay, right? Yeah, no, that's where I am." She looked at me watching her and shrugged. "Morgan's going to the city for a rock star thing," she finally said, after listening for a long time. Morgan's head snapped up and she narrowed her eyes.

"What's she asking?"

Hunter shook her head. "No, I don't know anything about that. Can you *imagine* her not saying? Come on. Yes. Okay. Yes. You too. Bye sis, love you."

"What did she *ask*?" Morgan said again, louder.

"I fucking heard you, and so did she, come on." They stared at each other for a minute, and when I realized neither of them was going to budge, I sighed.

"Hunter, why'd she call?"

"Well for one, like an idiot, I used the wrong card for the hotel. One that went to one of our joint accounts instead of just mine, so the bank alerted her." She handed the bottle back to Morgan. "And for two, she heard about some issues at some data centers and wanted to know if it was something I might know about, or if it wasn't related to anything and she was just paranoid."

Morgan laughed. "Your sister is too damn smart. I don't like her not being on our side."

"We're neutral," Hunter said. I waited for her to laugh, and she didn't.

"If you're neutral then what are you doing here?" I asked.

"The *Coutards* are neutral. *I personally* am on Morgan's side."

"Kinda like starting an LLC so that if the company goes bankrupt it's not you personally, it's the company."

I looked between the two of them. "But. You're the company."

"Not in the eyes of the law," Hunter grinned. "Basically, don't worry about it, it's fine. You worry too much, Allie. Also, we have a little bit of bleach left and I don't think it dried out yet, can I pretty please bleach a streak in your hair? I've got the itch now."

"A streak in my hair," I repeated.

"Yeah just...a couple inches wide." She held her fingers apart to show what she meant. "Look at what a nice job I did on Morgan's. Even with the box dye."

"You did do a nice job on Morgan's," I admitted.

"Okay good. We'll make Morgan pretend to be people and go wait for our dinner, and I'll put a streak in your hair and then put it in French braids. No, the other one. Dutch braids. So the braids stick out."

"Okay?" I'd never had anybody do anything like that before. "Are you just trying to make me feel included? Because—"

"Allie shut up and let Hunter play with your hair."

"Okay." Morgan tossed the towel from her shoulders into the bathroom and started to walk towards the door. "Morgan, you're still not wearing a shirt."

"God you're such a prude," she said, laughing, but she came back for her t-shirt.

"We're not totally done with hers, but there's only so long she can stay still and be fussed over," Hunter said, once I was sitting on the closed toilet and a section of my hair was laid across a piece of foil.

"I'm amazed she stayed still long enough in the first place. Whose idea was bleaching her hair like that?"

"Like, today, or in general?"

"In general."

"Hers, I'm pretty sure. She wanted to separate herself from the family look."

"That sounds like her." She must have done it when she ran away, I thought. I tried to remember how old she said she was. "Have you always known each other?"

"Oh yeah. Rachel used to come to talk politics with Mom, and Fran and Ardith were like the apprentices, and me and Morgan were the fuckups who wandered off and did our own thing." She folded the foil over my hair. "There isn't any good way for you to ask, so I'll spare you. We don't have an age thing in my family, the way yours does. It's our hearts that go, and that's unpredictable. Sometimes they just don't, even."

"Does every family have something like...that?"

"Considering it seems like the Wards are just assholes, I don't really know."

"I'm sorry, I shouldn't have—" I shouldn't have asked another question. I should've been more sensitive to what she just told me. But Hunter was like Morgan and that meant she was unpredictable too. I wanted to ask about her father but honestly that wasn't anybody's business.

"Don't worry about it," she said. "It's all fucked up anyway, right? We're people who turn into wolves."

"From the outside, it seems pretty impossible," I said.

"You've had a huge learning curve. I don't even know how I would've handled it, if I had a normal life for as long as you did, and then got thrown into this." She offered me the bottle, drank more herself when I shook my head.

Sure, a normal life. "And now everything else besides." I finally considered the implications of how empty that bottle was. "Should we check on Morgan?" For all I knew, though, it was Hunter who drank more of it. Neither of them seemed any different than when we got here.

"She's fine," Hunter said. The elevator dinged down the hall, and if I recognized Morgan's new stride, then Hunter definitely did. "See?"

"Just fine."

# Chapter Eleven

hile Hunter rinsed my hair and then braided it, Morgan fed her french fries and read comments off the video of the livestream. My job was to sit still on the end of the bed and drink my milkshake. When Morgan asked if I'd wanted anything, I didn't actually have a choice. They'd already ordered.

"I can't believe I slept all day," I said, as Hunter snapped the elastic onto the end of my second braid.

"Guess you needed it," Morgan said noncommittally. Meaning, she wasn't going to talk about it. Meaning she did know why, and it probably had to do with having pesky human feelings about killing a person not even a day ago.

"I guess I did," I said, since she was staring, daring me to say something else. To try and get into that kind of a conversation with her. "So are we going into the city tomorrow or on Saturday?"

"Saturday, first thing. Today and tomorrow is for just rest and recuperation," Hunter said before Morgan could open her mouth. "We drink, we smoke, we order food, we nap as needed, we watch bad movies on the tv, and that's it. No athletics, no gymnastics, nothing else."

"Did Morgan know that before right this second?"

"I think she's catching on," Morgan said to Hunter.

"I think she might be," Hunter agreed, picking up her milkshake. "Oh and you can try on the clothes I bought too. And I bought you both boots because I am very tired of the workboots look, or more specifically, that particular work boots color."

"Thank you," I said, surprised.

"Well I had so much fun shopping for you last time, Allie, I couldn't stand to leave you out. Plus you have to blend."

"Oh my favorite." I didn't know how I was going to blend with music industry people, but also thought that maybe it would be easier than blending with wolves has been. I'd worry about it when I got to it; after all, it was Morgan who was going to be on camera. I got up to look in the clothing bags.

"What kind of boots?" Morgan asked suspiciously, opening the next bottle.

"Well I got Allie something more fashion just for fun, unless you decide that you absolutely just have to have them. Otherwise, lace up timbs, just black. I know what you like."

"You sure do," Morgan said with a low laugh.

"Stop it," Hunter said, but she was laughing too, and I knew if I said anything they would definitely be laughing at me instead of just maybe.

I did and didn't know what rock star clothes would mean in this scenario, but it was mostly variations on Morgan's usual jeans and a t-shirt theme. Some of the shirts were longer muscle tees, with pictures or symbols on them, and the jeans were mostly straight legged, and there were some new sport bras but also some black lace bralettes and I hoped they didn't notice me blushing when I thought of Hunter shopping for Morgan for these things. Even though it was early summer, there was a cropped black leather jacket with a bunch of zippers, and a worn-in denim vest with patches on it.

The 'fashion' boots that Hunter said were for me were still fairly plain, and serviceable, which was good. They just laced up a little higher, and had grommet and lace accents on them, nothing I thought Morgan would like but nothing that was going to make me uncomfortable to wear. "And I'll do your make-up, Allie. Morgan, will there be somebody at the studio to do yours or...?"

"I love that you think Neil both asked that and communicated it to me." Hunter threw a french fry at her, that she opened her mouth like she was going to catch but it was way off. "This place won't have a makeup department, no. We played there once before."

"Okay I'll do everybody's makeup then."

"Oh, you don't have to worry about me," I said a little shyly.

"You don't understand, she loves this shit. If she could be bothered to maintain employment, it would be doing stuff like this. Makeovers, personal shopping, whatever."

"Why would I bother to maintain employment? It would take me away from youuuu." Hunter gave a little howl and dramatically tipped over on their bed. I had a moment where I wondered if, last year, Hunter was with Morgan when she got arrested. If she had been, Rachel wouldn't have brought her back to the house, so that Morgan could just hang out with her girlfriend when she was supposed to be in trouble. Something else I wasn't going to ask.

"You're ridiculous," Morgan said, but she was smiling, pleased in a way I hadn't really seen her.

"I am," Hunter agreed. "And now we should ridiculously choose what we're going to watch until we fall asleep. If we fall asleep, Allie might just be up all night."

"I hope not," Morgan and I said at the same time, and Morgan laughed.

· · · ·

WE WERE GLAZED IN FRONT of a superhero movie marathon, the room lit only by the tv, when Morgan's phone buzzed. It was honestly the longest that I'd heard awake-Morgan go without talking, and she and Hunter were a casual tangle of limbs on their piled-up pillows, like when the dogs slept all piled up on each other. Morgan twitched, though, and lazily brought her phone up in front of her face.

"Who is it?" Hunter asked muzzily, so I guessed she'd fallen asleep.

"Luke, if you can believe it."

"Sending you love notes?" Hunter teased.

"Shh," Morgan said, glancing at me. She frowned when she saw I was looking. "Well, I guess the cat's out of the bag."

"What?" I asked.

"Well, I guess the cat's still in the bag," Morgan said, giving Hunter her phone.

"I'm sorry I doubted you." Hunter squinted at the phone. "This is very tame, Morgan. Practically proper."

"I know, it's a damn waste of my time."

"Doubted what?" I asked.

"You have to assume he lacks experience texting, ahem, *ladies*," Hunter said. She looked at me. "And I'm going to let Morgan explain. Especially since I couldn't believe she didn't already."

"Explain *what*?"

"I technically already did, once," Morgan said. I stared at her. For once, I wasn't going to let something go. "Actually you were pretty fucked up, you might not remember. When I came and got you in Alabama? And I said that the Wards were still going to help us even though Rachel pulled the plug?"

"And you handcuffed Luke Ward in the back of a car or whatever," I said.

"Yeah." She waited, and I didn't say anything, and she sighed. "Well a deal's a deal, right?"

"You're talking about how you said you'd have a baby," I said, and then felt my face flush completely. "Oh."

"There you go."

"*Morgan*!" I said.

"Jesus, what? Which part?"

"We're doing this and you're. Well you can't get pregnant right now, while we're doing this!"

"I'm not gonna get fucking pregnant at all, but Luke is obviously not aware of that." She looked at her phone again, maybe trying to decide how best to answer, then looked at me again. "Don't tell me that I need to tell you about birth control."

"No, you don't," I said. I'd been in real school long enough for that, anyway. And even if I didn't, I thought I'd rather learn it from the internet than Morgan.

"Thank God." She typed something, handed her phone back to Hunter. "Okay how's that?"

"It's okay, I guess. I don't know what he's expecting?"

"Neither do I."

"Wait so Hunter, you don't mind? That Morgan..."

"Has been, how do we put it delicately? Passing time with Luke? No, it's okay."

"I do feel dumb for not realizing," I said.

"In all fairness, you've been against a double header of strong painkillers and an evangelical upbringing," Morgan said.

"I appreciate you being fair," I said, my head spinning as some things made a little more sense. Why Morgan taunted Luke at the idea of him being protective. Why the topic of how soundly I did or didn't sleep came up. She hadn't mentioned the deal again because she assumed I'd just forgotten. That was why Bill was so cheerful. Gross.

"Oh yeah I forgot about that," Hunter said. "Somehow."

"It's 'cause I did such a good job in my crash course of how to act normal," Morgan said.

"Of course, what was I thinking," Hunter said, sounding not at all convinced.

"Luke isn't gonna be happy when he finds out that—"

"Yeah, we'll burn that bridge when we get to it," Morgan said, sending another text. "Who knows, maybe we won't even live through all this."

"You're so fucking *cheerful*," Hunter said, saving me from having to say anything.

• • • •

MORGAN SPENT A LOT of Friday on the phone with various bandmates, talking about setlists and the new song she'd promised. As she predicted, she talked to Vinnie for ten minutes or so, singing to him and then playing the primary melody on her electric guitar, that she had a teeny little amp for, and he called back an hour later with a drumline. "You're a saint, Vinnie," she said.

The rhythm guitarist, Hope, also called with questions, but she was also more laid back about it than Al the bass player. She was the one who asked what cover they were doing. "Oh, yeah, we'll close with that. It's that TV on the Radio song we all like? Wolf Like Me? Yeah, exactly, we did it in Baltimore. That'll be fine." She was watching my face when she said it, and laughed when my eyes got big. "Right, it's a great song? So you're good? You got my files and Vinnie's? Cool, awesome. See you tomorrow."

"Is that everybody?" I asked.

"Al's gonna call back at least one more time, maybe two, but yeah." She waited. She was expecting me to be scandalized, or protest.

"So you've covered that before? What else have you covered? I don't remember very many being on your car tapes."

"Let's see...More Human Than Human, Fell In Love With a Girl, Whipping Post, Renegade, Werewolves of London but that was just once, at a place where they wouldn't move the piano off the stage for anybody's fucking sets." She shrugged. "There's more, but I don't even know how many of those you knew."

"You play piano too?"

"Maybe we should teach you bass, and drop Al."

"Maybe *what?*" I couldn't tell if she was serious or just wanted to get a reaction out of me, but she definitely got a reaction. "I am absolutely not cool enough to be in your band."

"Well maybe not *yet*, you're a work in progress."

Hunter laughed. "Jesus, Morgan."

"What? Am I wrong?"

"You can't just say shit like that to people."

"Allie doesn't mind, she's flattered. Right Allie?"

"Umm...Flattered by the band thing, not the work in progress thing."

"Good enough. See?"

"I stand corrected," Hunter said. She'd already rebraided my hair, then pulled that out and used a flatiron and something flowery smelling to make my waves and curls act a certain way. She'd also tried out a couple of different makeup looks on me, starting out with very dark and dramatic eyeliner and eyeshadow that changed how I looked completely. When I looked at myself in the mirror in shocked silence, she cleaned it all off and tried again.

"What does Morgan's typically look like?" I asked. "Other than sunglasses."

"Well sometimes she does the first one, and other times she does nothing and this one is kind of the middle ground." Middle ground was eyeliner that was somehow magnetic, because she put it on my upper lids and then stuck fake eyelashes to it without any glue, more dark eyeshadow but also some silver eyeshadow, and lipstick dark red enough to look a lot like dried blood. There was other stuff that I didn't know the name of, but the me who looked back at me from the mirror was partway between me and Morgan. Maybe it wasn't so bad, to not look like me.

"I kind of like that on you, Allie," Morgan said, cocking her head. Hunter had straightened her hair before going to work on me.

"Okay, so that's Allie for tomorrow then."

"Don't I get a say?"

"No," they both said. Hunter reached out and adjusted a lock of my hair.

"It's just nice to be different sometimes. You'll see. How do you know what you like, if you don't try things?"

"I guess," I said, and she smiled.

"Fantastic. This is going to be fun!" Then she looked at Morgan, remembering what this was all about. "Mostly."

"Oh, I'm still gonna have fun," Morgan said, grinning hard.

"Now you have to stay still long enough for me to do your nails," Hunter said, getting out the next bag, full of rattling little glass bottles, and tools I didn't know the names of.

"I mean, I don't."

"No, they always do closeups of you playing, and I want your hands to look *nice*, not like you've been fist fighting Luke Ward for the last eight months."

"I only fist fought Luke Ward *once*." Hunter raised an eyebrow. "No, sorry, twice. But the other fight was other Wards."

Hunter looked at me in appeal. "Allie?"

"No, I think she's right. The once in the parking lot was the other Wards. So the first one with Luke after she got the bullet taken out of her, and then the one he started. Well he shoved, I don't think he punched her. Actually, I think she's been the one punching him each time."

"There, see," Morgan said smugly.

"What am I going to do with you?" Hunter asked.

"Well right now, just my *nails*, apparently." Morgan rolled her eyes, and she sighed, but she sat where Hunter put her, and held out her hands for her manicure.

"Okay don't be weird." Hunter glanced at me, and Morgan snickered. "Allie, I've got three different colors of red in that bag, can you pick one for me?"

"Red?" Morgan asked.

"Yes, like the blood of your enemies. My god your poor knuckles."

"They're fine."

"You always say that."

I didn't know how long the pre-painting process was, and hoped to escape the tender mercy of having my nails done. Maybe just making Morgan endure it would be good enough. I looked in the bag and pulled out the three reds; they looked almost the same to me, but the chunks of glitter were bigger in the darkest one, and that's what I handed to Hunter when she put her hand out.

"Red *and* glittery," Morgan said. "Actually maybe it will kind of look like blood."

"Have I ever steered you wrong?"

"Probably," Morgan said cheerfully, and they both laughed.

# Chapter Twelve

I'd never been on a train before, and there weren't many other people riding into the city with us on our particular train. That was good, I realized that there was only so 'in public' I was used to being anymore, and was very self conscious about whether I was acting like a yokel or not. Morgan would tell me if I was, no question. I realized once on the train that I'd also never been in a city before, not like New York, and I thought I'd do my best to keep that to myself. I just had to do my best to blend.

Morgan carried her guitar and Hunter carried the case with the pedalboard in it and I carried a duffel bag of extra clothes and makeup and things that Hunter wanted to have along 'just in case' and I couldn't tell if that was real or if she just wanted to make sure that I felt like I was contributing. Or give me a job to distract me, because the second we were off the train and in the brightly echoing station, more voices than I'd ever heard at once before closed in on me in a way that felt physical, and I stopped and hunched in on myself and Morgan grabbed my arm and pulled me along with them.

Out on the street was loud too, but the noise was less close-in; it wasn't trapped by walls and ceiling and bouncing back onto me. The smells, though. Wet concrete and coffee and garbage and the freshly printed newspapers and a bajillion people wearing perfume and cologne and lotion and having minty fresh breath and smoking cigarettes or vaping and car exhaust and buses and birds, the birds made me think of the chickens back in the pines.

We were walking briskly down the sidewalk and Morgan was chattering about Madison Square Garden and I didn't know what else and I was smelling the hot plastic of traffic cones and the river and so much metal, grating and fire escapes and bike racks, when Hunter looked at me and said "Oh, honey."

"I'm sorry," I said, smiling desperately. "It's...a lot. There's a lot." It's too much, I thought, but I couldn't say that. We were here, and there wasn't anything I could do about that.

Morgan huffed, and looked around. "Well there isn't anyplace for you to stop and sit unless you want to just park it on the curb, but I don't think sitting is gonna help anything."

"I don't think so. I don't know."

"I think we're just doing this wrong," Hunter said thoughtfully. "We aren't showing Allie the city in the best way, we're just going about our business."

"Yeah because we have someplace to be."

"And to think, she's just like this all the time," Hunter said to me. Morgan laughed. Hunter linked her arm through mine as we walked, and got out her phone. "Okay, we're going to get coffee at a place coming up, and porkroll-egg-and-cheeses. Well you two will wait outside and I'll pick up this order that I just placed. Isn't technology wonderful?"

"I don't know if I can eat," I said, my stomach giving a shaky roll even as I said that.

"Nonsense, breakfast is important." A dog barked at us, eyes white and teeth snapping, as its surprised owner struggled to hold the leash. "Okay, I need you to answer me this honestly, are you ready?"

"Oh here we go," Morgan said, rolling her eyes.

"How many times have you been totally freaked out and she just left you to work it out on your own?"

"Is this so you can make me sleep on the couch or something?"

"Shut up, Morgan. Allie?"

"She hasn't really," I said, trying to think. There was just so much noise, so many smells, it was so hard to think. "It was more like I didn't want to bother her with it."

"Hmmm," Hunter said, looking at Morgan, looking at me, and looking at her phone again. "Okay I guess that's fair. Maybe. Okay wait here." She went inside a restaurant. I looked at Morgan who was looking off down the street, bouncing her head a little. I felt like she was already in the performance mindset, or maybe she just didn't really have different mindsets, other than dangerous and more dangerous.

Hunter came back out to us and distributed sandwiches and coffees and Morgan started walking again so we started walking again. Hunter carried Morgan's guitar as well while she wolfed down her sandwich and drank her coffee in three gulps, and then Morgan took what Hunter was carrying. "Thank you," I said. The duffle bag was slung on a strap, I could manage just fine.

I sipped the coffee carefully and it was good, I guess. This process, getting the food and all that, helped ground me a little bit. A sudden chorus of car horns made me recoil and wish that I had ears to flatten against my head and maybe drown out the sound. Or a few years on stage in a loud band, to have damaged my hearing.

"Okay next stage, hold on. We're all winging it, you know?" Hunter finished her sandwich, frowning in concentration. "Okay, it's hard to know what to focus on, right? Or how to focus? Try to ignore smells, or sounds. Keep your eyes open because somebody is marching us to her concert. Think about your new boots. Are they comfortable?"

"They are. I'm a little surprised," I admitted.

"I know they're fashion boots, but I wouldn't steer you wrong. I can kind of feel my eyelashes, with this mascara, that's kind of weird. Oh wait, don't pay attention to that. Okay. I know you've never worn an outfit like this before, is it okay?"

"Don't call attention to the clothes, she'll freak out about how her bra is showing," Morgan said.

Hunter closed her eyes briefly, took an elaborately deep breath. "Morgan. My love. My light. My fire."

"Yeah?"

"Fucking stop." Morgan looked at her, glanced at me, smirked a little.

"Sorry, Allie."

"My bra is supposed to be showing," I said. I'd never worn black lace anything before, or jeans that looked this tight but had so much comfortable give, or a shirt with armholes like this. Never, Mama would never countenance such a thing. It was so far beyond the pale, I couldn't even imagine what she would say about it. Morgan was still looking at me and I grasped for something else, something to pull me away from Mama's voice. "It's called fashion."

Hunter laughed, delighted, and Morgan did too, a little. "Well excuse the shit out of me."

"There, good, yes. We should've gotten you some kind of perfume, just something very light, maybe that would've helped as a front line. Morgan, give me a cigarette."

"Should've gotten pepper packets at that restaurant," Morgan said, complying, and Hunter made a face at her.

"I don't smoke," I said.

"I don't care," Hunter said, leaning forward so Morgan could light the cigarette for her. "I'll smoke it and you'll walk next to me and Morgan is barreling ahead because that's what she does, and we'll make it to the radio studio or wherever the fuck we're going and inside there will be normal and less people and," she waved her cigarette hand, "everything."

"I would walk *with* you if—"

"It's fine, Morgan, it's part of the patter. You're so *sensitive*." Hunter gave me a conspiratorial wink.

"Arguably, I—Oh they must've gotten here early, they got a spot on the street right in front of the place."

"Who...oh the van?"

"Yeah, that's Vinnie's van." She laughed, walking faster, and I didn't really realize why until a little guy with dark hair, smelling strongly of cologne, crawled out from under the van with a cymbal in hand. I was a little disappointed that the van didn't have album art or anything on the side of it. It was just plain white, kind of dinged up and rusty in spots, but the kind of van you saw bands use all the time in movies and shows and things.

"Can you fucking believe Al just left me here after we dropped the kit?" He asked.

"I can, actually," Morgan said. "Do they not already have drums inside?"

"You know, I thought of that after I dumped my kit in the street and before picking it up." He grinned up at her, and then looked at me and Hunter. "Hey Hunter, and...Morgan 2? New Morgan?"

"She's my cousin," Morgan said. "Allie."

"Well hi Allie, nice to meet you," Vinnie said. "Other than when her mother bailed us out of jail, we've never seen a member of Morgan's family and assumed that she hatched from a Jersey Devil egg or something. Like, she mentioned a sister? Maybe? You're cousins? You look a lot alike, wow. I guess I should check on the drum situation inside before I carry this shit in, huh?" He popped a fresh stick of gum in his mouth and went inside.

"Vinnie talks a lot," Hunter said to me in a confidential tone, finishing the cigarette. "Okay you ready?"

"Ready as I'll ever be," Morgan said, kissing Hunter on the cheek before going inside.

"She is just insufferable," Hunter said, but she was smiling, and we followed.

I didn't know what I thought a radio studio or whatever was supposed to look like, but it was very plain-white-walls office-y until we got back to where there was soundproofing and recording equipment, and yes a drum set, amps and microphones and all that. Me and Hunter were shunted off to one of the booth areas, where we could listen, but no noise we made would interfere with the recording and streaming. She looked at Morgan's instagram phone every once in a while, checking views and comments on the video, before queuing up the livestream that was happening just next to us.

I watched Morgan interact with her bandmates and the radio people. I'd never seen her in her element this way, driven and focused on something other than violence. She laughed and joked, but moved with efficiency. Checked the tuning on her guitar, did the sound tests, all of that, with the same easy confidence that I'd seen her break a windshield or cut a man's throat. I shuddered, and Hunter gave me a sidelong look, but then they were starting to play and she sat up to pay attention.

The first two songs, I recognized from Morgan's car tapes. One was the bonfire one that me and Hunter both got stuck in our heads, and the other was something fast and hard and loud enough that I still didn't really know many of the words. Then "Wolf Like Me," which I had never heard before, and it was a good song. It was also such a breathlessly obvious taunt, and Morgan absolutely reveled in that. It scared me, even though I knew it was on purpose. It was always on purpose.

"So you teased on Instagram two days ago that we would be hearing a new song today. I assume you saved that for last?" the host asked.

"Sure did," Morgan said, grinning, a little breathless.

"Do you want to talk a little bit about your songwriting process? I know you haven't been big on interview questions but, since we have you here..."

Morgan's eyes narrowed and I thought maybe she wasn't going to answer but maybe she just drew out the pause for suspense. "Process in general, or for this song? Well I mean, I guess they're the same. Everybody's seen that interview with Vinnie by now, right? How I have song stuff written on literally anything that comes to hand? That's because I like driving around so much. Road trip life, you know. Diners, rest stops, gas station food."

"How do you eat like that and—"

"No, we're not asking gross questions about my body, thanks." She grinned at him, hard, and he snapped his mouth shut and blinked a few times as Morgan noodled some notes on the guitar, maybe waiting to see if he would recover. "So anyway, I went and did that traditional rock and roll thing where I wrote a song about a crossroads. That might be what the song is called? Crossroads? Nobody knows 'til the record's printed." She glanced over her shoulder at Vinnie and nodded, and he did a three count with the drumsticks over his head and then they rolled into the new song.

I'd heard bits and scraps of it yesterday but now, really trying to listen, and hearing it in order and all the parts together, I felt like it was about us. Well not me, but the Morgan end of what we'd been going through. Everything going up in smoke, a desperate scramble to try to figure out why and how to fix it. Making a deal. It wasn't a screaming fast song, but it had a relentless, inexorable nature to it, and when it finished, it was on a grimly triumphant note. Well good, I thought. I hoped so, I hoped we'd get that payoff for Morgan, after everything. I'd spent all this time thinking about me and what I'd lost and gained and lost, I didn't spend a whole lot of time trying to see anything from Morgan's perspective, and maybe I should have.

There was a moment of actual silence, and then the host said "And again, we were in the studio this morning with Howling. Morgan, band, thanks for being here, you're always welcome. You can look for their new single, maybe named Crossroads, and this tends to mean a new album is on the way. Let's hear it for Howling." The people in the studio clapped, and one of them howled and Morgan threw her head back and howled, and then the ON AIR light went off and people took off headphones and exited booths, and went to clean up and unplug things, and talk to the band.

Hunter packed up the phones and looked around to make sure she didn't drop anything. "Okay, we'll see how that does," she said. "What did you think?"

"I like her music," I said.

"It'd be even worse torture around her if you didn't," Hunter said. I followed her out of the booth. Morgan was taking her guitar off and putting it in its case, one of the sound guys talking to her with his trailing-cord headphones hung around his neck, and all the voices were just one murmur together for me, which wasn't great but wasn't overwhelming at least.

The word 'party' came through to me loud and clear, though, and Morgan's eyes snapped to mine and she waved me and Hunter over. "Alright, we have choices to make," she said

"Do we?" Hunter asked.

"Yeah, we can go to a party right after this—yes Allie I know it isn't even lunchtime don't interrupt—and then when that winds down, go to a further party just across the bridge with this fine gentleman and the rest of the techs, or do we bum around the city for awhile and just go to the later party?"

"I assume you're even asking anybody because you're worried about what, food supply issues? Whether the booze will hold up?"

"Something like that," Morgan said. "Hey Vinnie, can I stow my gear with you?"

He made a show of gripping his chest. "You're trusting me with Excalibur? I don't know if I can handle the responsibility. I don't know if I'm worthy."

She laughed. "Look, you fucking nerd, it's that or it's carry it all the fuck over the place today and also to one or two parties, and I don't want to do that either."

"Oh well when you put it like that. What a relief."

Al gave him an irritated look. "We didn't plan for any parties," he said.

"Why, do you have somewhere to be?" Morgan asked.

"I wasn't going to stay all day."

"You can ride home with me," Hope said quietly. I wondered how many times she'd tried to be peacekeeper between Morgan and whoever. I also wondered why Morgan would keep Al around, if she obviously thought he was such a pain. Though maybe she'd been serious, when she talked about using me to replace him, and it wasn't just part of her patter.

"Hope gets carsick, she never drives with me if she can help it," Vinnie said to me in a confidential tone.

"I *only* get carsick when you drive, you maniac." She was laughing, though. The ribbing was good natured.

"You can't let other drivers take advantage of you! They smell your fear."

"Sure they do, Vin."

"What did we decide?" Morgan asked, edgy, ready to go. Hunter looked at me.

"I don't know if I can do two parties," I said.

"Okay, so we won't do two parties. Let's blow this popsicle stand and we'll figure it out." She exchanged numbers with the radio people, and Vinnie led us back out onto the sidewalk, air drumming as he went.

"I gotta go see my grandma while I'm up here, so I'll meet you at where for the party?" Vinnie asked. Morgan and Hunter put the stuff in his van and she forwarded him the address. He waved when he pulled away, and I waved back.

"Okay, Mary Poppins, what're we doing now?" Morgan asked.

"Central Park. Hot dogs and hot pretzels."

"Central Park is—"

"Yeah, I know, and we're walking because otherwise you're going to go into orbit or kill somebody."

"Sure, but what are you punishing Allie for?" Morgan looked as innocent as I've ever seen her, and Hunter laughed.

"The exercise will be good for her too, it's like tiring out a puppy so they can use their brain."

"Hey!"

"Sorry, Allie." Hunter made an apologetic face as Morgan laughed, and they linked arms, and we started walking back up-town.

# Chapter Thirteen

Hunter's exercise tactic did help me a lot. We kept walking, and walking, and we walked around Central Park and we kept stopping at street carts and buying more food, and walking more, and then eventually the sun was setting and it was time to go to the party, which I knew I was woefully unprepared for but couldn't think about that any more than I could think about the millions of people in buildings all around us, all living and breathing and moving and making noise.

Hunter took pity on us and let us take a cab to the party, but she spun it to seem like it was just part of the New York City experience, taking a cab, so it had to be an actual yellow cab and not one of the app-based things.

"Did you eat enough? Do we need to stop anywhere?" Hunter asked, sitting between me and Morgan. "Oh, should we bring snacks? Morgan?" Morgan was looking out the window, not paying attention. Maybe she was writing the next new song, or maybe she already had the whole next album sketched out in her head. Apparently there was just no way to tell, until the music came out.

"If you want snacks, I guess," Morgan shrugged.

"Won't there be food at the party?" I asked.

"Not unless you count edibles, I don't think, which I know you won't." I blinked at her. "God you're such a lost lamb. No there won't really be food, yes we can stop. We don't want to be nerds and be the first ones there anyway, we want it to be kicked off already. Entrenched."

"Snacks then? Or real food? Oh let's get ramen." Hunter leaned forward and gave the driver new directions. I didn't know how both of them could be like this and not just be fighting all the time, but it seemed to work out.

We were deposited on the sidewalk in front of a ramen shop and once again, Hunter went inside without us, but left Morgan holding her purse. "We could sit here," I said, looking at the tables.

"Mmmm," Morgan grunted. I wondered if she was just living in anticipation now, assuming somebody from Silvernail could try to grab her at any moment. Trying to be the right kind of prepared for it, maybe, so that they could take her without her doing too much damage and keeping the plan from working.

Hunter came back out with bags of takeout containers, and set them on one of the tables. "Okay, we can put everything together and kind of slurp while walking, or just eat here. We should eat here, I don't want to be a mess."

"Of course not, princess," Morgan said. "Here take your purse. What's in this thing anyway, rocks?"

"Aww, sorry my purse was too heavy for you, honey, I'll have Allie hold it instead next time."

"It wasn't...that's not what I mean," Morgan said, comically baffled, and for once I was laughing at her, and not the other way around.

"Just eat your ramen, and I'll worry about my purse," Hunter said. She winked at me, like I'd have any idea, but even though she'd had me get stuff out of her purse, I never noticed it being particularly heavy, or not. Maybe I just didn't know how heavy it usually was, and Morgan did.

When we finally made it to the party, it was unlike anything I'd seen before. Maybe in movies, or music videos. I didn't know how Morgan could stand it, but she loved it, there was no confusion there. She didn't have to keep herself turned down, here. Everybody was drunk, or stoned, or high, everything was larger than life. It was after sunset when we got there and just walked in, and though if we'd arrived earlier it would've been too early, it seemed like we got there in the middle of things.

It was dark except for strobing lights, or candles, or strings of Christmas lights. The reek of alcohol and cigarette smoke overwhelmed me, though not as badly as the train station had, and the music was so loud that I couldn't hear it, just the bass replacing my heartbeat with an asynchronous thud.

People were writhing, or dancing, just everywhere. I tried to keep up with Morgan and Hunter as they threaded through the crowd, I was always trying to keep up with Morgan, and I lost and found them about six times going from the front of the house or apartment or whatever this was to the kitchen at the back, where the drinks were, where some food was. Vinnie was supposed to be here, but who knew if he was already, or if he'd been and gone, or if he was coming later.

"Have a beer, Allie," Morgan said, holding a bottle out at me and then taking it back abruptly. "Wait no, I know you hate beer, hold on. They'll have something actually nice for once." I blinked at her, looked at Hunter, who shrugged.

"I don't need anything," I said, and Morgan glanced at me and shook her head, grinning, pretending she couldn't hear me. She inspected the garden of liquor bottles on the counter, picking a few as she went, then dumped some of each into a plastic cup at the end of the line, looking like she was using the lines on the cup to measure, before filling it up with a can of coke.

She took a sip, considered, added more from one of the bottles. "Here, try it," she said, shoving it at me so that I had to take it or wear it. My head was pounding, all of me was pounding, from the soles of my feet in my borrowed boots to the top of my head, and Morgan wasn't going to leave me alone until I took a sip, so I took a sip. I tasted coke, and sweet, and spice, and waited for the burn which didn't come and took another sip, confused. "Right?" she yelled.

"Make me one," Hunter said, and Morgan obliged, and then they were on the move again. People recognized her here, but I didn't know if she knew anybody. More than once they looked at me standing nearby and did kind of a double take. She was going to see that as a missed opportunity, a joke we could've taken advantage of. If even the Wards mistook us for sisters, these party people weren't going to have a chance.

I sipped my drink very slowly; my senses were all already befuddled by what was going on, I didn't need to get drunk too. Morgan didn't share this thought, obviously, because even though I'd never seen her drunk that I knew of, she was drinking pretty freely, and smoking like a chimney. At one point, somebody pulled her aside, showed her something that I couldn't see. She laughed, all flashing white teeth in the dim-bright light, and bent to their hand for a second. When she came back up, she rubbed her nose with the back of her hand, and then saw me looking and made a face. She shoved back over to me.

"What is your *problem* we are at an *industry party* and keeping up appearances," she snarled or sneered or both.

"Did you just—" I stopped myself from saying the painfully wide-eyed, 'did you just do a drug,' and she watched me struggle with too-bright eyes burning into me. I needed her to understand that even though this party was nothing like the one Kyle attacked me after, this party was too much, I wasn't going to be able to cope with it much longer. And Morgan needed me to understand that, in spite of everything, she needed this. Maybe because of everything.

"You gotta stop being so uptight," she said after a minute, shouldering into me. There was no way somebody who wasn't a wolf could hear what we were saying. "I'm fine, this is fine. They need to think that I'm relaxing too much, that I'm *vulnerable* and that they can take me."

"I guess," I said, biting my lip. I was always too slow for Morgan. Morgan, who killed two people when we got Rachel out. There was only so vulnerable those people were going to trust her to be; that was probably why they'd come loaded with silver, after.

But no, they'd shot Dulcie with silver. At least one of them had come loaded with it all along.

"Finish your drink and if you want I'll make you another one in a little while. Try to have fun for once in your life. Mingle."

"I don't know how," I said, hating my plaintive tone.

"Yeah you do. You'll be fine." And she went back to Hunter, who maybe also had done a drug, and there was a break in the music and then somebody, somewhere in the building wolf howled and I couldn't keep myself from looking at Morgan, but she laughed and threw her head back and howled back in answer and then the next song came on and I realized it was hers, it was a Howling song, it was okay, they were fans, they knew her music. Some of them, she'd met before. That was why we were there. I'd heard her tapes, I'd heard Howling howling. That was a thing they did, they did it on the radio just this morning. She'd gotten sunglasses from someplace and she was everything I wasn't, and I basically found a wall to stand against and be out of the way and slowly drink my drink.

People came up to me a lot, thinking I was her, and I played a game with myself where I tried to see the exact second they realized that they were wrong. A lot of them then immediately lost interest, if I wasn't Morgan then I wasn't worth the time, but depending on how drunk they were, they stuck around a little bit, asking questions. Mostly nice, just curious how cousins could look so alike. I told somebody I was a stunt double, and somebody else that I was a body double, but I didn't know how much they believed me, and eventually I wandered back to the kitchen to pour my drink down the sink, because when I got to the bottom, it *did* burn, because it wasn't like Morgan actually mixed anything.

There was bottled water, and I took one of those, and realized how tense I was only when the seal cracked and I relaxed a little bit. I knew that we were setting the trap this time, but knowing that didn't do anything for my nerves. Then I made myself even more nervous by realizing that I'd let Morgan out of my line of sight and went back into the darkness and flashing lights to find her, and she spotted me from across one of the rooms and yelled "Allie there's a karaoke machine!" And I wished I'd stayed in the kitchen after all. At least there was just the one overhead light there.

"Make Hunter do it," I said, as she fiddled with the screen.

"No way in hell," Hunter said, smiling happily. "It'd cut this party's throat if I sang on the karaoke."

"The karaoke," Morgan repeated, snickering.

"Morgan I don't want to," I said.

"But, unlike Hunter, you *can*," she said. "Do you know 'Under Pressure'?"

"Oh Jesus you are not making me sing 'Under Pressure' in front of all of these industry people at your industry party."

"Well you're no fun anymore." She looked at me over the tops of her sunglasses. "You're really gonna make me do this alone?"

"You're the lead singer in your very own band."

"Yeah but—" She stopped, considered. "What if I wanted you in the band too?"

"You keep saying that, but you don't want me in Howling." I wasn't fun enough, I didn't have to say. Maybe I was still more fun than Al.

"You don't know that."

"You're only saying it so I'll play your reindeer games."

She looked down again. "Well, it's 'Under Pressure" or "Despacito.'"

"I don't know what that is."

Hunter laughed and said "That's the saddest thing I've ever heard. Alexa, play Despacito." They both laughed and I stared at them and Morgan shoved one of the microphones in my hands.

"You'll be fine. It's not real."

"Morgan, I—"

Staring at me through her sunglasses, she pressed play, and the people who'd been paying attention to our bickering let out a slurred cheering. Then the front door slammed in and there were lots of bright lights and people yelling "POLICE" and the party people just kind of wordlessly yelling and Morgan grabbed one of my arms and Hunter grabbed the other and they started towards the kitchen at the back of the house except Hunter was hurting me, my shoulder not as healed as I'd been thinking and hoping, and somehow I wrenched loose of Hunter, making an awful, involuntary noise that I could hardly hear for everything else happening, but Morgan kept hold of my wrist and we got to the kitchen, and then out the back door into the walled patio that they had and what was a wall like that to a trio of wolves? Even with my shoulder. Morgan gave me a boost and then we were all back on the street and mingling with the people in the streets, Morgan lighting a cigarette and passing it to Hunter and lighting another one for herself. She even still had those sunglasses on.

"Nothin' like a late-night sprint to clear your head," she said, and we all laughed, still tense and hyped up, but relieved.

"I wouldn't have expected anybody to call the police on a party in this neighborhood? I didn't think we were all that bad," Hunter said.

"Yeah who knows." Morgan looked around with a sort of 'now how the fuck did we get here?' look on her face. "Yeah, no. Feels weird, actually."

"Oh, was that different from other parties you were at that got broken up by the police?" I asked, holding my shoulder and trying to catch my breath. I should've still been wearing the stupid sling.

"You're such a nerd, Allie," she said distractedly, looking at her phone.

"That's me." She looked at me, and I grinned hard and toothy, scared and hurt and angry, and she punched my non-hurt shoulder, not hard.

"I guess we just need to find another party. What a shit-show."

"You always think there's another party," Hunter said. She was weaving just a little, but that was the only way I could tell that with her drinking, anyway, she couldn't quite keep up with Morgan.

"Yeah, 'cause there is." Morgan stuck her phone in her pocket, looked up to orient herself, and then we were on the move again. I didn't know what time I thought it was, and it didn't really matter. We passed the side street still full of flashing police lights from the party we'd fled, and a few people had gathered to try and gawk at that, it looked like. There were also a couple of ambulances idling on the street, which I guess probably were needed after police raided a party for no reason.

I started to ask Morgan how far it would be to the next party when I smelled the lightning, and I had a moment to think that I didn't know it was supposed to rain before I grayed out.

• • • •

BUT IT WASN'T RAINING, I knew that. I didn't smell rain, or hear thunder, and somebody who was too rough about my shoulder kept me from just falling straight on the ground, but I made some kind of sobbing noise and I could feel them pause. Then I was laying down on something hard, but not the ground, and there was a sudden pinch on the inside of my elbow. I've never been in an ambulance before but somehow

I knew I was in an ambulance, or something like it, before I opened my eyes..

My eyes didn't want to open, and they didn't focus when I got them open. It was so bright. I didn't recognize anybody around me, not by what I could see, and not by what I could smell. Where was Morgan? Where was Hunter? My elbow was cold, getting colder, where it pinched. Somebody pulled my shirt back off my right shoulder, and an indistinct voice said "Subject confirmed." and even as my panic rose, a thick darkness came and dragged me down.

# Chapter Fourteen

I had an eternity of bad dreams. Flashing lights and yelling and the taste of pennies and throw up in my mouth. I heard Kyle's beery whisper in my ears. The smell of my face pressed against dirt. The burn of silver, the shock of a bullet. My face pressed against still-warm asphalt after sundown. Morgan's eyes catching light. Hunter's freckles.

I woke up.

My hands felt all tingly, my everything felt all tingly, and I tried to sit up or roll over or move, stretch, anything, and I couldn't. I couldn't move, I was pinned to something soft-ish, and I dragged my eyes open. It was a white room, a far too bright white room, and there were lots of machines around. It looked like the movie set of a medical facility, where they weren't really sure what most machines in a hospital were for and so figured more must be better. My head felt cottony and my sinuses stuffed up, and I opened my mouth to try to call out, and was overtaken by a yawn instead that popped my ears and cleared my head somehow all at once and I was inundated with the sharp, sharp disinfectant smell and immediately transported back to the Silvernail facility we got Rachel out of.

The machines were all whirring or clicking or beeping and at first it was all very overwhelming, like when I was on day three of trying to reconcile and figure out that I was a wolf, and what that meant for me, how I was supposed to live like that. Or like when we got to New York City this morning. I also felt like my wolfness was sluggish, like I was reaching for all of those much stronger senses that I knew were there, and there was a piece of glass between me and them.

I thrashed, tried to sit up, and became more aware of what was holding me down, of leather cuffs on my wrists and ankles, chains rattling on bed rails. What felt like belts across my belly and across my forehead. I pulled against them in a not-yet-panic, confused about where I was and what was going on, testing how strong I thought they were, testing how I thought they were attached, and then I realized there was another person in the room, another sharp smelling person but a human not a wolf or anything, who had medicine with them, and a laptop? and a gun. Or was it two people, one with a gun? I tried again to open my eyes, and it worked better this time. The room was so white, so bright. AC turned up way high.

"I'm too cold," I said. Morgan would've sounded better, I thought. And I pulled against the restraints again, because Morgan would. I rolled my eyes around to look for the other person I could smell. They stood off to my right, out of reach. A woman, her hair pulled back severely, not holding a laptop, holding a tablet, I was close. A man was by the door, that was where the gun was. Something else, though. He smelled familiar. I remembered his scent from Mama and Daddy's house, and remembering that *did* make me fight the restraints again, harder, until I twinged my shoulder and exhausted myself, sweaty all over even though I was cold.

The way the woman watched me was uncomfortable. She was maybe trying to behave at a distance but that was a front. I couldn't tell if she hated the sight of me, not actually human, or if she hated that she was employed by people who kidnapped folks to do medical experiments on, the way Annie had gotten scared, or what. Maybe she just had something for dinner that wasn't setting right, who was to say.

I didn't know at all how I should act and I felt like maybe the Ward family had like, team building exercises on what to do if you were kidnapped and interrogated and experimented on but the Culvers sure didn't. So I didn't know. Should I fight it? Should I go along with them, to a point?

"I'm going to take your vitals," the woman said. I wasn't wearing my clothes anymore and had a sick feeling in my stomach about that. These people had undressed me. They knocked me out and took me here and undressed me, put me in a paper gown, strapped me down.

I still had my cross on, I could feel that. I wondered if they somehow thought it was silver, and that their drugs worked good enough, and that they'd have a warning if something went wrong for them. I wondered if they gave me what they'd had Mama give me all along, and that worked to keep me from being a wolf, until it didn't.

I was so scared, almost as scared as I'd ever been, but I was angry too and getting angrier. Don't change, I thought. That's what they focused on with Rachel. Don't change. Don't change. "Do you have rabbits here?" I asked, which didn't really make sense but I was only able to stay focused in little bursts, the room fuzzy and also in weird sharp focus.

She ignored me, though, like she was reciting a script. "If you don't cooperate with me, we'll have to drug you again and wait until you wake up again. The process will be repeated as long as it needs to take in order to successfully take your vitals. Do you understand?"

"I don't want you to do any of this. I don't want to be here. You don't have my permission for this." Permission wasn't the word. I couldn't think of the word. Like it was going to stop them. But if they were recording this, I didn't want there to be any confusion about my cooperation.

She didn't say anything to that either, though, just stepped to the side of the bed and put her fingertips against the inside of my elbow, counted. She put a thing against my neck until it beeped, my temperature. She looked at various machines, made a couple of entries, then set the tablet down and took out a thing that looked like a pen until she clicked it and a light shone out the bottom of it. "Remember what I said."

"Please stop doing this. Why are you doing this?" A whine crept into my voice, and I thought maybe I was slurring anyway. She waited, looking at me and I stared back. It was hard not to bare my teeth at her, but I didn't have the practice Morgan did, making it look like an aggressive smile. It would've just looked like a terrified snarl, what it actually was, and I didn't want to do that either.

Of course she wasn't going to answer my questions. She shone her bright light into my eyes, first the right, then the left, then the right again. "Open your mouth," she said. I thought about what it would take to make them pry my mouth open, and then I did it slowly, so slowly I heard my jaw crack. I spent time in front of a mirror with my mouth open after all of this got started; my teeth looked like people teeth. We're people until we aren't people anymore. We're stronger, faster, have better senses and better reflexes, but we're people for all intents and purposes.

I remembered Morgan or maybe it was Sela? Saying "It ain't exactly science. We're people who turn into wolves."

"Am I gonna live, doc?" I asked, trying to channel Morgan. Was Morgan here too, somewhere? I hoped like hell, I prayed to God, that they didn't get Hunter too, just me. Me, who knew the least. Me, who they probably knew the most about, thanks Mama. Even if I was only a subject number, for the medication they gave me. They knew, they'd known for years. They knew what was happening with me even before I did. What an enraging thing that was. They knew more than me, about me.

But the tracker was on Morgan, they were supposed to get Morgan.

But they knew about me. I was already their subject, and I'd gotten away for a while. But now they had me back. And without the tracker, Morgan would never find me. Had they just always wanted me back?

The woman finished whatever she was doing on the table, poked at one of the machines, and my veins filled with ice. I hadn't even noticed the IV, and couldn't protest, before my eyes were dragged shut again and I floated away for a while, into a dark world of whispers and medical smells and Morgan telling me to keep my shit together and I prayed. They killed Dulcie and they did whatever they'd done to Mama when she asked, and they hurt some more of us real bad, but I prayed that I could endure this. And that somebody would come for me.

• • • •

"I'M GOING TO TAKE YOUR vitals."

She didn't wake me all the way up this time. It did not make me more cooperative. "I don't want to be here. You can't keep me here." I sounded very loud in my own ears, my voice angry and raw-edged.

"Open your mouth."

"No." She moved in anyway, with the thermometer, and I snapped at her almost without knowing I was going to do it. Don't change, Allie. Alleluia. Control yourself.

The woman gave up arguing with me and hit the button that controlled the IV.

· · · ·

"I'M GOING TO TAKE YOUR vitals."

"I do not consent." That was the word, consent.

"Noted." It was a man this time, in scrubs, with the tablet. The man with the gun was the same. The nurse glanced at him from time to time, maybe wary, maybe curious. The other woman didn't have the nerve, I thought. Or she hated the sight of me that much, like Mama.

My head wasn't restrained anymore, for some reason, but the rest of the restraints were still there. I pulled against them, not as hard as I could, just a chain rattle amount. They weren't comfortable but they weren't hurting me. I imagined what it would feel like if they'd chained me to a hospital bed with silver chains and I felt a little shiver. It would be torture, almost unimaginable torture. Like when I accidentally grabbed the handle of a cast iron frypan when I was little, not realizing it was hot. Like when I walked home to Mama after the party and then took the silver spoon ring off my thumb because it was itching me and then it was burning me. I still had a band of smoother skin around my left thumb, not scar colored, not thicker than the rest of my skin like other scars I'd gotten in my life, not raised like the bullet scar in my shoulder was shaping up to be. Just...smooth.

The thermometer beeped, and he took my pulse, all of that, not looking down into my glare. I imagined that I was staring hot and angry and threatening like Morgan, but I probably just looked like I wanted to cry. Because I did want to cry.

"We have some questions for you, Allie, while you're awake. Your mother didn't do you any favors, interrupting your care with us. We're concerned for you, and your brothers. Do you know where they are?"

"No," I said, which was true, thank God. I felt like maybe I'd have a hard time lying. A harder time than usual, trying to lie. "I was never in care with you. I always saw the pedia—" No, I couldn't handle that word right now. "Dr. Reynolds."

"When is the last time you remember taking your...vitamins, Allie?" I wondered what they really were. His tablet would tell me.

"I don't know," I said. Did I know? I kind of knew. "Before the party."

"The party you attended in New York City?" He sounded confused and I laughed, too slowly and off key. I heard Morgan saying New York City in that funny voice.

"No, the football party. School." I'd taken them that day, maybe. Or the day before. When I'd started public school, real school, even though I didn't ask anybody if their mama gave them vitamins every day, I kind of got the feeling that they didn't. I took them when Mama reminded me, because she watched me take them then, but even she forgot every couple of days. Was that why they stopped working? Or were they always going to stop working?

He made a note, I assume. "What happened at the school party?"

"Not a school party. After. Football."

"What happened at the party, Allie?"

"No," I said. I'd told all the people I was going to tell, about what happened after that party. About what didn't happen. I was done telling people about it and they couldn't make me.

"If we don't know your history, then we don't know how to help you."

"I don't need your help," I said, spitting a little on the p. "I don't want to be here. Let me go."

"We can't do that. It wouldn't be safe." The man behind him with the gun shifted a little, the belt creaking. I laughed again; I wasn't the dangerous one. "You need to help us help you."

"No. You want to hurt me. You hurt me." I didn't know if the other man would know I was talking to him. I couldn't see him. But the nurse man pressed the button again, even as I said "No!" again, and I went to sleep again.

# Chapter Fifteen

T he next time I woke up, the man who stood staring at me wasn't in scrubs, wasn't holding a tablet. It was the man with the gun. He was older, in a suit that seemed very nice. The fabric had a soft sheen even under the fluorescent lighting of the hospital room or lab or whatever it was I was being held prisoner in. He didn't look like the kind of man who normally wore a suit, but I wondered why I would even think that.

I wondered how long it had been. It could be three hours for all I knew, or three weeks, or three days. My mouth was dry, just all moisture gone from it, and my eyes felt gritty. I felt stiff. I felt dizzy, even though I wasn't moving, like my head was a balloon that might float away.

"Do you know who you are?" His expression was neutral, in a schooled sort of way. He smelled like aftershave and soft buttery leather, and natural fibers. The gun. The silver.

"I know my name. Who are you? Why am I here? I don't want to be here."

"I'm sure you don't," he said with a short, cruel little laugh. Was this a Silvernail? Was this *the* Silvernail? I didn't know anything about the family. I barely knew about my own family, and my brain kicked at those little thoughts in a tiny panic, like a rabbit in a snare. He was the one who shot me, I was very, very sure. He was the one who shot Dulcie.

I took a deep breath, let it out slowly. I didn't have the restraint over my belly anymore. I still had a hospital gown on. I couldn't sort out what I thought it meant, that they were one by one removing the physical restraints. Maybe they were adjusting the chemical ones. Maybe they just planned to lobotomize me and have their own in house werewolf to poke and prod and experiment on, now that nobody expected me to be in public anymore.

I realized I'd been tensing myself up further and further as my thoughts twisted around on themselves, and my fingers had gone numb with the angle the restraints pushed into my wrists. The man watched this with what seemed to be some kind of detached interest, and I gritted my teeth together, breathed through my nose, counting breaths. Don't change, I reminded myself. Do. Not. Change. Not in front of this man, not here. Don't give them that reward, that satisfaction.

Don't give him a reason to shoot you again.

He waited, maybe for me to ask more questions, give something away without knowing I was doing it, and somehow I just looked back at him, calmly as I could. The drugs helped. Maybe they hadn't expected that, or even the just plain Culver stubbornness. He sighed almost inaudibly when he realized I wasn't going to say anything. "This will be more comfortable for you if you cooperate with us."

"I don't know why I'm here. I don't want to be here. Why do you have me here? When will you let me leave?" I just let myself whine. I was trying too hard to control myself otherwise, I could let myself have that.

"You have to understand, we don't think it's safe for the general populace for subjects like you to be at large," he said.

"I don't see as how you get to make that decision," I said.

"You're here now aren't you?"

I guess that was meant to shut me up, and I was happy to shut up. I still felt distant from everything, my thoughts, my body. I still felt like crying or raging. And I didn't know what I was going to say. Not like I could argue my way out of wrist restraints. But I might be able to break them. Wide leather cuffs that buckled like dog collars. Metal chains on bed rails. This man and I were the only people in the room.

As my head gradually cleared, I smelled more details off of him. His heart rate was elevated; not a lot, but he was excited by this conversation, these prospects. Maybe by the idea of getting to hurt me, or one of us, more. I stared at him and I waited.

He was looking at my face, still standing just out of reach. I began to pull very slowly on my left ankle restraint, so slowly that I couldn't even hear myself move, just eventually feel the tension. Feel the bed shift, minutely, and then also pick up the tension. I waited for him to notice, say anything, but he continued talking. For somebody who wasn't a wolf, he seemed really into power, and control, and authority.

Strength and balls, I heard Morgan say. She was always so angry.

"You understand, that even with the losses this project has suffered, it's impossible for us to write it off at this point. We know that you're out there, and it's our responsibility to the public that you aren't a threat to their general safety." I didn't know what he meant, I couldn't understand what he was talking about. All I wanted was to not be chained to a bed in a medical facility, about to be tested until the day I died. That didn't seem like too much to ask.

I wondered if there were cameras in the room, recording all of this in full color and audio, but if there were I couldn't tell. They didn't smell any differently from all the other machines. Maybe cameras were the only reason he wasn't hurting me for fun. Cameras and profits? He was saying something about what they could do with our blood, our DNA. Morgan had joked about super soldiers, maybe that was what Silvernail wanted. A nice Army contract, for super soldiers. I couldn't listen to him anymore, for the roaring in my head, was that my heart? I had to concentrate.

Don't change, I thought. The restraints would just fall off if I changed but no. I pulled slowly, so slowly. When the man turned his back to pace, I also started to pull on my left wrist restraint. I hoped the chain links broke before the bed rails did, but whatever. Whichever way it happened, I was happy to give it a go. What were they going to do, make me sleep again? Whatever. What the fuck ever.

I hated this man, I hated what he was doing. I didn't need to rely on Morgan's spirit, Morgan's anger for that, I had my own. I had my own anger, my own resentment, my own deep and abiding sadness, and my own strength.

Distantly, I remembered Sela talking about how stoned she'd felt, was that this? Was I actually doing anything at all, or just hallucinating it?

The man kept talking and I didn't listen to his words at all even though he was the only thing I could hear, other than the electricity and my own breathing and the machines beeping and then the slow, quiet groan of the chains and the bed. I stopped pulling for a moment, changed the angle just a little, very slowly, I didn't want to pull the bed apart, actually. I couldn't run away with parts of the bed hanging off me.

I was going to have to kill this man, I thought. Thinking that scared me, I was scaring myself, but I hated him and had to be strong enough and he wasn't sad *at all* that Dulcie was dead and he had killed her and I was going to have to kill him, maybe kill a lot of people, to get my freedom. I did it once, faster than I could think to stop myself. Now I was planning it. And God would forgive me, I had to think, because this thing he was doing here, this terrible thing, wasn't a God filled thing. He had a gun and it was loaded with silver and he was the one who shot me. Maybe he was the one who shot Daddy. He only wanted to hurt me. He only wanted to hurt everybody, me and Morgan and Rachel and Fran and Sela and Sidney. Sidney's baby.

Don't change. Don't change. Why was I thinking about God so much all of the sudden? If I thought about it, I could feel my cross cold against my skin. Or I imagined it.

"So I'll take you to show to your people," he said. He said people, not subjects or creatures or animals. "I'll take you and you'll cooperate, and your entire little pack or whatever you call yourselves will be able to be together again. Just under our purview. We already have it set up, how we will keep you and how we will treat you. I'm sure you'll be unhappy, because you're all stubborn like that, but there isn't any reason you can't be comfortable." He had his back to me for some reason, looking out into the hallway. Wait, who did he mean, when he said my people? They must've gone through my phone. Who was in my phone?

Morgan.

Rachel.

Maybe I should wait. I couldn't stop myself now, though. I'd get loose, kill him, open the door, get outside. Don't change in front of them. Don't give them anything.

I turned my head to look at him as I pulled again, as I felt the chain on my left wrist pulling apart like raw dough, slowly, so slowly, and only I could hear it, I was confident. He was looking out a window, like we were in a hospital ICU and there was a window looking out down the hall.

He was looking for the security people, I was certain. More than one would come, a bunch would come, they had to do their show of strength, show of force. They had to show how they had me securely, how they had overpowered me. I was going to show them. I pulled with my right wrist, both my legs. I knew how hard to do it now, how slow I could be while being quick.

I didn't know what this metal was, it was different from, say, the toy handcuffs Morgan bought. I wondered how strong they had been, how long it had taken Luke to get out. He had been angry, of course. It had killed just enough time, I was sure he was out of them before Morgan had even fully driven away.

Maybe. Maybe not.

My heart hammered in my ears and my back itched, my shoulder itched, my skin itched all over, and I had to stop for a second. Don't change. What was he saying? I felt all woozy, from the adrenaline, from whatever they put me to sleep with, all of it. Fear. Anger. Did they take a bunch of my blood, like they did with Sela? There weren't any IVs in here anymore, in my arms anymore.

"Your family has to recognize you, of course. They have to think you have been treated well."

"As well as you treated them?" I asked. I couldn't help it. My ankles were loose and I lay there as still as I could make myself. The leather cuffs were still on them but I could handle that. My left wrist was loose. My right wrist was almost loose. I breathed slowly, in through my nose out through my mouth, and he turned around just as my right wrist came loose, and I came up off the bed and had him by the lower jaw, had his face slam-pressed against the glass, before he could do anything but widen his eyes to see I was free.

He'd thought he'd have time to draw his special gun, if I got free. Special gun with special bullets just for us.

"We're going to walk out of here," I said, slowly to make sure I was speaking clearly, loose chain ends rattling. He was taller than me. He wasn't stronger than me. He tried to fight against me and he just couldn't. I'd spent so much time around only wolves, that I didn't realize how strong and fast I was. I hadn't had any time to try it out around normal people. I didn't realize that I was actually strong like Morgan. Fast like her, even drugged up like this. I'd crossed the room like that, and it felt like the top of my head caught up three seconds later.

He tried again to get loose and I slammed his face into the window again and wondered where the security people were, if there was a button he thought he'd be able to push to call them. I wondered if there was a hallway or an elevator or what. I didn't know anything, I just needed to get out of here.

I kind of hoped nobody had agreed to come. I hoped they'd put him off, that they were going to negotiate further, that they wouldn't agree to anything he said. I had an idea that they hadn't. Or it was going to be Morgan in the parking lot, with Ward snipers backing her up. She was going to have that 80s action hero rescue she craved.

I also had an idea that I actually shouldn't kill him. Killing him wouldn't help me. He didn't know that I couldn't stand to kill him, though. I should make him work for what he'd done to me already, should make him take me out of here. I wasn't smart like Morgan, couldn't get around keycard things, or locks, couldn't superhero my way through guards. Couldn't hardly think with the drugs, or not think smart, just in tail-chasing circles, working around to obvious solutions.

He was gonna be my guide and my shield. I used one hand and my weight to keep him pinned against the glass and with my other hand opened the straps on the cuffs on my wrists, let them fall to the floor with the rattling of open-linked chains. The ones on my ankles would have to wait, but I'd done it. I'd done the first step of getting myself free, with nobody's help but mine and maybe God's. Maybe it was just on my own.

"You can't just walk out of here," he said, and I took the end of his tie and jerked it over his shoulder so I could hold onto that and a handful of his shirt and coat at the back of his neck and use him to walk in front of me.

"Don't touch anything I don't tell you to touch. Don't yell. You're gonna walk ahead of me, and we're gonna walk out of here. Is this room door locked?"

"No."

"Okay. Open the door and we're gonna walk out of here. Do we turn right or left?"

"Left."

"Okay. Do that and I won't twist your head off." He made a noise like he was choking but I didn't hold him that hard. He was just furious, so utterly furious, that he of all people was in this position. A teenage girl overpowered him in her hospital gown, when he thought he had all the power, and started jerking him around like a puppet. Maybe it'd be good for him, a little bit of humility. Maybe it would make him more angry and he wouldn't care about studying us anymore, just about killing us. Who could say, I wasn't a fortune teller.

Nobody was in the hallway and I almost couldn't believe it, but it gave credence to my idea that this was where the trade-off was supposed to happen. Maybe it was supposed to happen soon, and the rest of the employees except for guards were sent away. Maybe Morgan was coming now, maybe my family was coming now. Maybe it was the only reason they woke me up this clearly, so they could lie about how they were treating me. Not like they were going to put me in restraints and put a hockey mask on me like Hannibal Lecter. Hannibal had gotten away too, though. I almost laughed, stopped myself, almost did it anyway.

I smelled through my nose with my mouth open, took a good deep breath. Lots of security down the hall, but none of them were too excited by anything. They were bored. They didn't know the agenda was right out the window. "Keep going to the exit. What's the next turn."

"A right, and then the hallway is straight."

"Any keycards?"

"On the next door we'll see."

"And?"

"That's it."

I smelled the truth on him. I guess it was probably against some kind of safety regulation to make an actual exit keycarded as well. Actually, probably, if I pulled a fire alarm all the doors would open anyway and I wouldn't have to worry about keeping control of him. Was there one? Had I seen one?

I imagined how the alarm would hurt my ears, how there would probably be strobing lights, and how bad that would be for me, even with the drugs making me and separate me. But it would be very confusing to those guards up there too. It would be very bad for this guy. I should've pulled his gun and dropped it somewhere. Maybe I should do that. Yeah, I should do that.

I reached for his holster, fumbled it a little, and he gave a startled jerk as I pulled the gun out.

Drop the gun? Keep it to threaten him with? Drop the gun. It was heavy, why were guns always so heavy?

I flung it away, back behind us up the hallway, praying it wouldn't go off accidentally. It wouldn't go far, I didn't think, but he didn't have it anymore and that helped me.

It was hard to think straight, my skin taut and humming, the wolf I wanted to change into was *right there* but I couldn't do that, not here. It was so close.

Was leaving him alive a mistake? He liked hurting us. He was so angry. He hated me so much. He wanted to make so much money.

I was so dizzy, what did he say about blood? They took a lot of Sela's blood. Did they take mine, or was this just drugs?

He was walking slowly, dragging his feet, and I gave him a shake and a push. "Keep walking, we're not out yet," I said in what I hoped was my tough Morgan voice. I peered around him down the empty hallway. There were double glass doors up ahead, with a red lit keycard next to them. Finally we got there, I still didn't smell anybody else, my feet were cold on the shiny white floor.

"My keycard is on my belt," he said.

"Good, you're good at following instructions. Pull your keycard, run it, and then give it to me." I heard him grit his teeth and smiled. Good, for once it's you in the hot seat, mister.

He pulled the keycard off of his belt, slowly, ran it, slowly, the light flashed green. "Open the door and hand me the keycard." He opened the door, held the card just over his shoulder. "No games, asshole." He held the card back further and I took it with the hand that held his tie, tightening it up on him for a second. "Walk." We walked.

As we approached the exit, I looked for a fire alarm. I could hear security now, hear them moving around, making preparations, bantering, laughing, talking. They sounded how the Wards did when they were getting saddled up for something.

"You aren't going to get out of here just like this," the man said. "There are ten men and women in that room, all prepared to take you and yours down. And where will you go, in a hospital gown? With nothing else? You don't even have shoes."

He seemed to forget I was a wolf. Wouldn't that be funny, if after all this they still didn't really believe it. I was grinning now, in anticipation, in fright, to keep from laughing. I felt kind of crazy, and it was hard to keep myself moving in a controlled way, not jerking him around, not running, just slowly walking down the hall. Not attracting attention.

"Ten, good to know," I said. There was the exit, there was the door to the security room, there was the lever to pull in case of fire. There was a fire alright.

God damn it, Morgan's bonfire song was in my head again.

I felt him tensing, taking a breath, ready to blow my cover, so he thought. If he couldn't shoot me, then his ten security men and women could.

I *yanked* on his tie, and that nice expensive fabric tightened smoothly on that nice knot he'd tied, and he made a *hrgk* kind of noise like a dog pulled up short on a chain, and I pushed him as hard as I could both down and towards the door to the security office, and wrenched the lever on the fire alarm so hard that I pulled it off in my hand as the alarm started braying wildly, the loudest thing I'd ever heard in my life, the flashing lights the brightest and then darkest, brightest and darkest. But I'd prepared for it, I knew it was going to happen, and I ran at the exit, slammed against the door, pushed through the door, ran barefoot out into the parking lot.

The asphalt was still warm from the sunshine of the day but it was quiet outside and dark and hardly any cars were there. I had no idea where I was but I kept running because even if this was a mistake it couldn't possibly be a mistake because staying there where I was would've been the worse mistake. I couldn't let them keep me, I wouldn't let them keep me, and I couldn't run in a straight line but I was running. The ankle restraints flopped on my legs but I was running.

I smelled Rachel before I saw or heard her, my ears were ringing, and she had me by the arms, had me in a fast embrace even as she turned to run with me, supporting me. It was Rachel, Rachel was here, even after she'd told us to never come home again if we left when we did, that last time. Rachel came for me.

There was a big open lawn, no fence here, and then trees a lot of trees and I could hear cars far away but I couldn't tell how far away because they seemed far and close at once and my senses were all weird even as they also tried to be hyper focused. But Rachel was here, she'd come for me, thank God Rachel was here, and we were running and the people behind us came confused out of the building, yelling but not knowing yet where to look, and I heard the man yelling, his composure gone. I imagined he'd probably taken his tie off by now, maybe gotten his gun back, or gotten another gun. I wanted to cry and laugh and scream and I ran and then Morgan was there too, coming from the side, shouldering into me once as a greeting, saving her breath to run. They had come for me, they both came for me.

The second we were out of the light, in the fringe of the woods, we changed, and we thrashed out of our clothes, and I kicked off the leather cuffs with their trailing chains, and we kept running. I hadn't changed since I got shot, and my shoulder was stiff and weird but I couldn't stop and maybe they helped me with all the drugs, maybe it helped me cope, gritting my teeth and following Morgan, who had never slowed down for me, not once. I heard gunfire, smelled the acrid burnt powder.

We ran longer than I'd ever run, as human or as a wolf. We ran until I couldn't see anything but Morgan's bleached skunk stripe in the night ahead of me, couldn't hear anything but my hoarse ragged breathing. I was gulping for air and getting less air every time, and all I could do was keep running, all I could hear was Rachel's sure strong strides behind me and feel the rhythm of my own footfalls and I concentrated on that, the rhythm of running and keeping up with Morgan, the rhythm of running and then Morgan was jumping over a concrete barrier on the edge of a yellow lit highway and I jumped, desperately and too early or too late, my bad right front leg slipping, I hung up on top of the concrete and tumbled onto my shoulder onto the shoulder of a road, scrambled to my feet, gasping, whimpering, gasping, tongue lolling as I stumbled and tried to start running again but where was Morgan? She'd been just ahead of me. I knew she was. There was so much light all the sudden and then I could only see light I could only see light and it was like I could *hear* the light the high pitched light, and then Rachel hit me from the side and knocked me off the road, onto the grass median, and there was a brief screech and the worst noise I'd ever heard, a high pitched screaming cry and a yelp together, and the smell of burning rubber, hot metal, and blood.

I staggered back to the road, cringing, heaving, my head and tail low. Rachel was a heap on the asphalt, her muzzle pointed towards me, she was breathing, she was breathing but she was glassy eyed and foaming. Her mouth moved but no sound came out as I bent my nose towards hers, and then Morgan scream-howled, louder than a siren, right in my ear, and when I flattened to my belly on the pavement she bit me, hard, on the back of the neck, and shook me, teeth gripping, scraping, tearing, dragging me to my feet. Once I was up she shouldered into me, pushing me away from the road. I dragged my lips up away from my teeth, but I was so tired, I was so overwhelmed, still so drugged out from whatever they just kept putting me under with, and Morgan ran into me again, and again and I could only turn and run, cringing, her driving me ahead of her like a rogue lamb returning to pasture. We crossed the other highway lanes, no lights no cars, the grass turning to asphalt and then another concrete barrier to leap over. It was only when we were in the woods again that I heard people start to shout. Did I hear Hunter? Maybe I just wanted to hear Hunter. She could save Rachel. Oh God. Oh Lord, save Rachel.

Me and Morgan kept running, kept running, through woods, through somebody's backyard where a dog startled up from sleep but was too slow to catch us or even bark at us until we were gone again, until we came to a gas station parking lot with a pickup truck in it, Luke and Joe waiting for us, Joe's face dead serious as he opened the back door for us and we jumped in and collapsed on the seat while Luke drove away in the night, his lights off until we were a mile or more down the road, then lights on and driving faster than he should, a radar detector standing sentinel on his dashboard, Joe talking on a phone with somebody. I didn't have clothes if I changed back, only my cross, the chain tangled in my fur. I was so tired, so sick and dazed. The adrenaline left me, the anger that sustained me left me, and I put my nose against Morgan's neck and fell asleep or passed out, still as a wolf. I didn't know if I'd stay that way once I was asleep and I didn't care. I couldn't handle anything anymore and everything went dark while I was still breathing hard, my toes spread to shed the heat from all that running.

# Chapter Sixteen

I woke up with the prick of a needle in my arm and tried wearily, clumsily, to thrash away, panicking that they found me again that they caught me again, that I never actually escaped, but Luke was so much stronger than me, it was a joke. "You're safe now. That's the wakeup drug," he said, slow and clear, and I thought maybe he'd been saying it for a while. Maybe even before he injected me. Once it got through my thick thoughts I stopped fighting him. The wakeup drug. Okay. That was okay.

The truck was parked. It was still nighttime and we were in a parking lot. I was remembering things in flashes, remembered the screech of tires, remembered Morgan's teeth, remembered that wolves didn't wear clothes, and I wasn't a wolf right now anymore, but I had a blanket around me. Covering me.

"Can you walk?" he asked, and Morgan shoved past him impatiently. She had clothes on.

"It doesn't matter." She got me to my feet and bodily held me up, walking me into the room we were parked in front of. Joe was in there, just finishing a phone call. Luke followed right up behind us, closing the door. She sat me down on one of the beds and roughly got me into jeans and a t-shirt, ignoring my whimpers and protests. If I actually whimpered and protested, I couldn't tell if I was just frozen.

Then she turned and put her hand through the wall.

All things considered, we ought to have been thankful she didn't punch a stud and break her hand. As it was, I just sort of sat on a bed all drawn up into myself, feeling like my nerves were electric wired and there was a storm coming, but I couldn't think straight. I didn't know if it was the drugs or if it was Rachel or if it was my own inability to control myself. My head was all fuzzy and everybody's voices were very loud and very distant, like somebody yelling into a microphone but what they were yelling wasn't words that I knew, wasn't a language I knew. Maybe if I stayed very still and small, what was happening won't have happened.

I about jumped out of my skin when Joe touched my shoulder, and I couldn't keep from crying out, in surprise or fear. Everything felt bad right now. I looked past him, looked at Luke and Morgan. Luke had stepped in close to Morgan, put his face in her face, because those kinds of things made a normal person back down and regroup. Morgan didn't budge an inch and stood there with her nostrils flared, staring up at him. Her hands were clenched and there were a few drops of blood on the floor. I think he kept her from punching the wall again at least. And she didn't punch him. For once.

"Rachel?" I asked, quietly, because I didn't know what to ask, how to ask. The screech of tires came to me again and again, the noise she made when the car hit her. The back of my neck itched and I put my hand to it, dried blood crumbling against my fingertips from where Morgan bit me. I hadn't had that before, gotten injured while I was a wolf. Maybe somebody should look at it for me. I couldn't find the words to ask. And I needed to know about Rachel.

"We haven't heard from Hunter again yet. We know Hunter picked her up." Joe stopped for a long time, or maybe it wasn't a long time, and I looked at him. "She was alive when Hunter got her."

"Thank God," I said, and even if she didn't hear the rest of it, Morgan heard that, whipping her head around, shoving Luke aside like he wasn't anything to come get in my face.

"Thank God? What are you thanking God for Allie? Creating these fucking assholes who want to experiment on us like they're goddamn Nazis and we aren't even people? Thanking God that me and Mama were there for you, kept being there for you, and now you're okay and she isn't? Is that what you're thanking God for? That you're here? You selfish little bitch. I wish you'd never been born. I wish your stupid mama killed you when you were a baby. Or killed you the night she brought you to New Jersey. Fuck you, Allie. Fuck God." It was the only time I'd ever seen Morgan cry. Now, when it was Rachel in danger, maybe dead, her eyes were laser focused, she was mad as hell, and she was crying and Luke was trying to pull her away and he was having a hard time doing it without just bodily scooping her up.

"Hey now," Joe said mildly, putting his arm around me. "It isn't Allie's fault they grabbed her instead of you, and it isn't Allie's fault that they drugged her all up. It's amazing she did what she did, you can smell it coming off her, can't you?"

"I can smell it, don't you worry your fucking self about that. This is so *fucking* stupid." But she backed off of me, at least for the moment, knocking Luke's hands off her. She paced in a tight circle, flexing her hands. Fingers closed, fingers open, fingers closed, fingers open. Blood going drip, drip, drip off her hand. I looked at Luke, who for once didn't seem smug or angry, just tense. Frustrated. He looked at me, came over. Joe's arm was still around me and I leaned into Joe, away from Luke. I was tired, so tired. I couldn't pretend that Luke didn't scare me, the way I should've pretended, the way I always had to try to pretend, and he stopped before he was looming over me, crouched down to talk.

"We aren't staying here for very long, just wanted a place to regroup that wasn't the truck," he said. "We'll be moving on soon as we get the call from Bill."

"Okay," I said, because it seemed like I was supposed to. Behind him, Morgan stomped into her boots and then stomp-limped into the bathroom, and I heard the water running. The wake up drug wasn't really making me feel as awake as I might've hoped. As anybody might've hoped. The edges of everything were still blurred, and my thoughts were only sometimes swimming up to me.

"Allie listen to me." I pulled my head around and looked at Luke, it was hard to look at Luke. "I know Morgan just got you dressed, but we need to check you over."

"I'm okay," I said, because no, I didn't want Luke 'checking me over.'

"You're not, and we need to get a handle on that. And make sure that they didn't have the same idea as us."

"What?" What idea, I didn't know anything about any ideas.

"We need to make sure they're not tracking you," Joe said. Joe sitting still, with me against his side, just waiting. He had the ability to be very quiet, very still, very patient. Morgan came and leaned in the bathroom doorway, watching with her face set and her arms folded.

"They didn't just let me go," I said. In protest, or out of pride.

"I know, we know, but Rachel had a chip, and they didn't think she was going anywhere either," Luke said. I heard Morgan grit her teeth when he said Rachel, but he looked at me steadily, moving his head to keep my gaze when I wavered. "So just let me look at your back. Your back and shoulders, if nothing else. Your neck, where you're bleeding. Can you do that? You know we don't want them to find us." He was trying hard to be good and steady and not threatening, I thought. He was trying very hard. If somebody tried to tell me that Luke could try this hard, I wouldn't have believed them.

Just my shoulders. Back and shoulders. I was panting again, everything welling up around me again, the world doing a slow tilt-spin. Just my shoulders. That's where they chipped dogs, right? And it was where they chipped us. They didn't think we were people, that man said so. I didn't want a chip in me. I didn't want I didn't want

Luke snapped his fingers in front of my face. I breathed in, breathed out. "Okay," I said. He was asking, he could've just done it. We were all trying.

Well, maybe not Morgan.

Joe let go of me slowly, and moved out of the way. I pulled up the back of my shirt so it was around my neck, scratching against the bite there, hunching over onto myself, and Luke stood behind me, first just looking, the flashlight from his cell phones casting weird shadows on the floor, and then he dropped it on the bed and pulled the shirt out of my hands and down, moving my hair away from my neck, where the blood was. "What is this?"

"Morgan," I said, trying not to jerk away from him. I closed my eyes. I felt like things were a little steadier if I closed my eyes. I didn't know why my shoulder didn't hurt. My collar-bone.

"Joe, washcloth." I listened to Joe cross the room, slip past Morgan, run the water, come back. Luke dabbed it a little too firmly at first and I hunched even further onto myself, my breath caught in my throat. "Sorry." The washcloth wasn't too hot, wasn't too cold. Joe got the water just right. "It could be worse, but I do think you need stitches."

"Okay," I said, because it seemed like he wanted me to say something.

Then he touched my left shoulder blade, almost in the middle of my back. His hands were very warm, but I couldn't stop myself and flinched from his touch, and from the sore spot he'd poked. "Yeah, there it is."

"Get it out," I said, panic clawing at my throat, black spots in my vision. "Please, please get it—"

"Luke, give me your knife," Morgan said, straightening up.

"I've seen the way you cut your steak, I'll do it," Luke said. He had? When?

"Is that okay, Allie?" Morgan asked. She'd never asked me anything like that before, I couldn't answer her, I just nodded too hard, swaying. Why did they wake me up, they should've done this before they woke me up. They should've let me sleep and sleep until everything was better again. I could've just

"You think you can stay still or should Morgan hold you?"

"I don't know." I could feel them looking at each other over top of me.

Morgan came and crouched, gripping my hands in hers. "Squeeze when it gets bad," she said. "You probably can't hurt me."

Your hand is still bleeding, I wanted to say, but that thought ran away. I leaned forward more, my head against her shoulder, and Luke put one of his warm hands on my back, his fingers framing where I could feel the little lump. He sniffed once.

"Okay, then." It hurt, but not as much as I expected. His knife was sharp, and his hand was steady, and I was thankful for both of those things. Mama always said to be thankful. He didn't cut for very long, and then he put the tip of the blade against where he'd cut, which felt like a scratch but was burning harder as the seconds passed, and he must've given a little flick while squeezing, maybe like getting out a splinter, before he said, "There's the fucker." He held his hand over my shoulder; it was a microchip all right, about the size of a grain of rice, but not exactly like the one I pulled out of Rachel. Probably this one was broadcasting.

"Give it here, I'll flush it," Morgan said, pulling her hands out of mine. Did I squeeze? I didn't remember. Her hands were red. My hand had her blood on it. I wiped it on my jeans. The jeans I was wearing, I didn't know whose jeans these were, whose shirt this was.

"I got it." He went into the bathroom. The toilet flushed, and the water ran. He was washing his knife, I thought. They put a chip in me, I thought. They drugged me and put a chip in me and

"I'm going to put a bandaid on that," Joe said. "And then pull your shirt down."

"Okay. Thank you." I wanted to take the blankets and crawl under the bed and wrap myself up in them, maybe stay there for a hundred years. Except I wouldn't live a hundred years, none of the Culvers would, and the way that thought just snuck in there made me burst into tears.

"Oh come the fuck on," Morgan said, but she threw her hands up in to the air instead of punching something again, and I put my face in my hands and tried to be as quiet as I could so that I wouldn't make her more mad at me. It was the kind of crying I couldn't stop, the running nosed, hot-teared, raw-throated sort that just made me even more dizzy and disoriented. I cried and Joe sat down with me again and hesitantly rubbed my back.

Luke's phone rang and I tried to stop crying, holding my breath. He looked at it, shook his head. "It's Bill," he said. Hunter wouldn't call him anyway, I thought. Hunter only called Morgan. "Hey." He listened for awhile, holding the phone to the side a little so Morgan could hear, saying uh-huh every once in awhile, then hung up. He looked at her, and she nodded. "Alright, we're moving out."

"Joe, will you take that duffel out for me?" Morgan asked.

"Yeah, okay," he said, sounding a little confused. He picked it up, and Luke tossed him the truck keys.

"Get it started, we'll be right out." I watched them do this, feeling detached, like this was a movie and they were actors. Everything just had such a dreamlike quality to it, such an unreality. I just couldn't get my head straight, couldn't make myself get up to follow Joe out. Normally I would do that. Morgan came to my side, like she was going to help me, get me to my feet again and walk me out to the truck again. Luke was on my other side and Luke had the flash of another needle in his hand and he said, "You'll feel better after this."

"No," I said, trying to scramble away from them, sick with fear, panic. Betrayal. "No, don't, please don't, I don't want—" but Morgan already had me from behind and Luke already had my arm, and they were both so much stronger than me and the needle stung and the needle was cold, and I was cold, and

# Chapter Seventeen

I woke up with my head pillowed on a hoodie on Joe's lap, and it was daytime, but that was all I could say about it. The radio was on, but not loud enough to matter, just a smear of white noise. Mild talking voices. A long long string of station identifiers. Morgan and Luke both smoking cigarettes up front, their windows open enough to suck most of the smoke out.

I looked up at Joe, who was looking out the window, but he looked down at me when I moved. I realized I was holding one of his hands. Clutching one of his hands, in a death grip, and I made myself loosen it up, silently mortified. How long had I been doing that? How long did he let me do it?

"Allie's awake," Morgan said, her tone completely flat.

"Did we—"

"No, we didn't hear anything," she said, jamming her cigarette into the ashtray.

"How are you feeling?" Joe asked me.

"I don't know." Luke gave a short, quiet laugh at that, and I felt very small. I also didn't know how I was going to gracefully sit up from how I was laid across the seat, but after thinking about it for probably a little too long, I put my feet down first and kind of came up naturally, Joe supporting me. "A little sick. Mostly tired. Cold." My neck hurt. The AC was blasting and I didn't really understand why.

"You might be detoxing," Luke said. Which while factually important, was anything but comforting.

"Oh shit, baby's first detox," Morgan said.

"Oh good," I said faintly. Detoxing. And I'd never purposely done a drug. "How long did they have me?" I asked. I couldn't let myself wind up for too long, I couldn't pick my words too carefully, but I had to know and nobody had told me.

"Two weeks," Morgan said shortly. "Well. Ten days." She turned in her seat to look at me. I didn't know what to think, or what to do with the information, now that I had it. Ten days. I lost ten days. They had me for ten days. They didn't wake me up ten times, I didn't think. I just remembered two, before the one where I escaped. Three total. No, four.

"Ten days," I said, to say something. That was so long, that was too long, but any amount of time was too long. "And since then?" Since you drugged me again, I wanted to say but couldn't say. I couldn't believe they would do that. Maybe I shouldn't have been surprised that they would do that. Morgan would do whatever it took, always.

"Just last night," Joe said, holding out the hoodie to me, helping me shrug into it. "It's afternoon now, around two thirty." Morgan looked at him and then turned to face forward.

"Where are we going?" We had to be going to wherever Hunter took Rachel.

"Right now we're putting distance between where we were and where we are," Luke said.

"But—"

"Shut up, Allie," Morgan said, lighting another cigarette. I looked at Joe and he made a face and shrugged.

"And we'll have a medic look at you," Luke said.

"No." He looked at me over his shoulder, frowning.

"What do you mean, no. Your neck is torn open, I had to perform jackknife surgery on you in a fucking motel room, and you're coming off ten days being drugged into oblivion and them doing god knows what else. You're not going to just walk that off."

"I'm done being looked at," I said, too loud. Too brittle. "And I guess if you need to hold me down and drug me again to make that happen, you will. Because otherwise I need to be able to not do that right now. Not be poked and prodded and *handled*." My voice shook on the edge of tears but I got it out.

"Okay, I get that, but let's maybe consider that you aren't making the best decisions right now." Luke sounded like he wanted me to know how patient he was being. Not how sorry he was.

"I said no. That should be good enough."

Morgan lit another cigarette. "She does have a point," she said in a bored voice. She kept clicking her phone screen on, like she could possibly miss a text with it in her hand.

"Fuck you, Morgan," I said, I think surprising all of us.

"Allie—"

"You *helped* him." How could she? She knew how awful that would be for me, for an apparently still-growing list of reasons.

"I helped him to help *you*, dummy. I don't know how you thought you were acting, or how clearly you were thinking, but you weren't acting like you'd make it to your next sentence, much less back out to the truck."

"You knew that would happen! Why did you wake me up anyway!" I was starting to sound hysterical, I thought, and then realized I probably had all along, no matter how justified. But when we got Sela out, and Rachel, neither of them had to run miles through woods and across a highway, and I didn't know if they could have. I didn't know how I did, however badly.

"Because it's easier to get clothes on an awake person. Because we thought you'd wake up better than that."

"Sorry I can't be you. Sorry to disappoint you once again." There were better insults I could fling if I was more clever, but I could still sense even that getting a rise out of her. I didn't know why I was fighting with Morgan instead of Luke. I mean, I knew why I was fighting with Morgan. Especially because Morgan would rather fight than talk about anything approaching a feeling.

"I think we're getting away from the point here," Luke said. "We're going to make a pit stop and then keep going, how does that sound?"

"Thank you," I said. Walking around even a little bit would probably help me feel steadier, I thought.

"I'm fine," Morgan said, even though that wasn't really what he was asking.

"Regardless." Luke turned off the radio and Morgan turned it back on again. "You're not going to hear anything you like."

"You don't know what I like," she snapped.

Where we stopped was the kind of place set up like a food court with restaurants, and gas pumps outside. Morgan was out of the car and partway across the parking lot before I even got my feet on the ground, and I wondered if I looked as dazed as I felt. Joe stuck with me, obviously determined to both keep an eye on me and also be unobtrusive about it. "Let's hope she doesn't kill somebody in the women's room," he said with fake cheerfulness.

"I don't know, maybe it would improve her mood," I said. I wasn't sure I was joking.

"I'm sorry," Joe said.

"You don't have anything to apologize for." What was he going to do, if Luke and Morgan were united on something?

"There just isn't anything better to say. About any of this. I'd ask you if you were okay but I don't want to know what it sounds like when you say yes to that right now. Because you would anyway, I think."

"Yeah, I would." I thought about it. "I'll stop lying that I'm okay if you'll stop saying you're sorry for stuff you didn't do."

Joe blinked at me. "Yeah, that sounds good," he said slowly. I stuck out my hand, and we shook on it, and Morgan came back past with sunglasses I didn't remember her having, and a giant drink.

"What are you nerds doing?" she asked, but her heart wasn't in it, and she went back to the truck without waiting for protest or answer.

We split off to the different echoing restroom corridors and even though it wasn't crowded I still felt like there were too many people there. I dithered for too long about what stall to use, closer to the entrance or further, and then I spent too much time washing my hands, just watching the water run over my fingers. Just feeling the water. If anybody had given me a new phone, Morgan would've texted me to see if I fell in. As it was, when I got back to the food court part, Joe waited pretty anxiously there for me.

"Vanilla," he said, handing me a milkshake.

"Yes, but—"

"I figured you might not be hungry, but you should probably have something."

"You're right," I said, blinking away tears. I was so surprised,
maybe way too touched. Still detoxing, as Luke said. That made
sense, with how tired I was again already, how detached I was.

I fell asleep more than once in the back of the truck, waking up alternately with my head against the window or against
Joe's shoulder. He didn't say anything about it, just let me go,
and I was thankful for it. Thank God for small blessings. I
couldn't bring myself to just lay down on him again, but also
didn't know what was stopping me.

It wasn't hard to believe Morgan maybe really did wish Mama had killed me. It was hard on my heart, but not unrealistic.
On the other hand, she was as pissed as I'd ever seen her, as worried as I'd ever seen her, and Rachel was the way to get under
her skin, I knew that for a solid fact. I prayed for Rachel, but I
prayed without real hope. I'd smelled her blood, and our noses
had almost touched. I don't know if somebody could be hurt as
bad as she was and live through it.

And still, a lot of things were blurry and confusing. Why
haven't we heard anything about Rachel? What we were supposed to do next. Was there a next or were we just waiting
again? We were in a hard spot, because bored and angry Morgan was dangerous, but it was also dangerous to expect her to
follow a plan right now. If Luke was smart, he'd know that.

When we stopped again, it wasn't at a camp or a motel, it
was another Ward house. I was relieved to be done driving for
the day but also I was so tired, the thought of putting on a polite face to be somebody's guest made me want to crawl under
the truck and sleep there on the street. The thought of Morgan

being exposed to new people she hadn't met before, while expecting to play nice right now, was actually harrowing.

"Whose house is this?" I asked, because nobody was asking.

"Mine," Luke said.

"Oh, no shit?" Morgan asked, as if she'd only just made contact with the idea that Luke lived somewhere. Maybe she had. I know I did.

"I'm not here much, my neighbor has keys to make sure things are okay. I texted her that I was coming, so she wouldn't call the cops."

"Her?" Morgan half teased, but Luke didn't take the bait, just led us inside.

It definitely smelled like nobody had been here in a while. Not bad or even musty just... empty. The front door opened into a living room, with couch and recliner and TV mounted on the wall, and straight back from there was a kitchen, and what looked like a hallway.

Luke gave a sniff. "No matter how many times I tell her I don't like brownies..." He dropped his duffel in the recliner and went into the kitchen, the rest of us following him like ducklings. There was a foil-covered pan of brownies on his stove, and a note on the counter that he picked up and glanced over before stuffing it in his jeans pocket. "Beers in the fridge, if you want 'em. Water. I don't have much food on hand, but there's menus in the drawer there." He looked at me. "See? No medic. But I still think your neck needs stitches, and while I can do it for you here, I don't really know that you want that."

"Why not? I can't see the back of my neck anyway," I said, and Morgan laughed.

"Atta girl." She got a beer out, twisted the cap off. "Which drawer?" Luke pointed, and Morgan shuffled around with the papers, brought them to the kitchen table, sat down. I felt like I was shaking a little, like those little dogs that always shook. I wasn't cold, I just didn't know how to stop.

"Suit yourself, I guess. I've got spray lidocaine in my kit here, that'll help." Luke disappeared into his house, leaving the three of us in the kitchen.

"Have you been here before?" Morgan asked Joe. "This isn't just some weird movie set?"

Joe blinked. "Yeah, I've been here."

"Because it almost seems like Luke hasn't been here before," she said, spreading the menus on the table like a hand of cards.

"He's stayed with Bill a lot since coming back," he said. That means he's been where Joe was, too. "Helps with family stuff."

"Where are we?" I asked, and Morgan only moved her eyes to look at me.

"Pennsylvania," Joe said. "West of Philly."

"They got a place with gigantic sandwiches," Morgan said.

"And fried green beans," Luke said, coming back with a kit that he set on the kitchen table. I watched him get stuff laid out; I'd had stitches once before, I'd been told, when I was too little to remember it myself. I was a toddler in new shiny Sunday shoes, and tripped on the altar steps at Daddy's church and banged flat on my face. As the story went, Mama carried me wailing and bloody from the church, put me in the car, and drove me to Dr. Reynolds's house, and he stitched me up at the kitchen table, much like this. "Can one of your hold her hair out of the way?"

"Joe can, I'm ordering food," Morgan said, getting up with the menu and her phone.

"You don't even know what we..." Joe trailed off as she walked away.

"I'm sure it's fine," Luke said, frowning at his needles. "Let's just get this done."

"Thank you," I said.

"First I need you over the sink while I flush this with saline. Do you know when your last tetanus shot was?"

"Um." I bent over the sink and tried not to flinch too hard both at Luke's proximity and the cold liquid. I needed all those vaccines when I finally went to real school. "Like two years now?"

"Good." He turned all the lights on in the kitchen, frowned more. It was interesting, how businesslike he was being. "I guess that's good enough."

I sat down at the table and leaned forward. I had my hands on the table at first but I could feel them shaking, and tucked them into my lap instead, before Joe said anything as he hesitantly gathered my hair out of the way. Both of them looming over me was hard to deal with, and that on its own was almost distracting enough, even before Luke sprayed on the lidocaine, put gloves on, and started stitching. Morgan banged outside, probably to smoke, since there didn't seem to be any cigarette smell in here, and I didn't even jump at the sound. I was either too used to her antics, or too deeply frozen in place.

"Almost done," Luke said at one point. He had to realize that I was about to shatter apart. "You're doing good."

"Thank you," I said automatically. I didn't feel like I was doing good, but it was nice of him to say so. I was staying very still, anyway. Maybe that was all the good I needed to be right now.

"I didn't stitch everything up, just the two big deep and long ones on each side. You'll be able to take those out in about a week, I guess. You watch, we'll run into a medic and they'll tell me I shouldn't have done this at all." He pulled the gloves off and stepped back. "Okay, you're done."

I felt like I could breathe again, and I sat up slowly. "Thank you."

"How's that feel?"

I started to say okay, then looked at Joe and remembered our handshake and actually thought on it a second, moving my neck a little bit. "Kind of tight, kind of scratchy, but I think it would've felt like that anyway. Maybe this way my head won't fall off." I tried to smile.

Luke laughed a little, shaking his head. He threw the gloves away, moved the garbage back across the kitchen. "You Culvers," he said, and I didn't know if he meant it as a blessing or a curse. As if summoned, Morgan came back through the front door, rattling plastic bags.

"Dinner is served," she said.

"I didn't know they delivered," Luke said.

"They don't." She started to put the bags on the table, looked at the kit there, put them on the counter instead. "Don't look at me like that, your truck is entirely fine. Also I saw your neighbor, and I told her that you were helping us out by letting us stay here a few days, and we're your nephew's friends. Joe's your nephew right? Yeah. So your reputation with her is unsullied."

"Morgan…" he said, maybe picking which thing to hone in on.

"Not like I'm gonna be around forever, Luke, you gotta keep your prospects open." She grinned hard, and her eyes were so bright it was like they left traces when she moved.

I heard him take a breath, let it out. And then he said, "Unless the thing Fran did worked."

"Yeah, we'll just wait around twenty seven more years to see if it did." Another intake of breath, because I think maybe she said more years than he expected, but then she frowned and cocked her head. "Oh we're so stupid. This might've worked anyway."

"What might've worked anyway?" I asked, when Joe and Luke just stared at her.

"This harebrained scheme of mine. Allie, did they take your blood?"

"I don't know. How would I know?" I thought about how dizzy I was, still was. "Maybe? Probably? It would make sense, with how they treated everybody else."

"Oh shit maybe we did it."

"Morgan, what are you talking about?" I was so tired of everything happening around me, and to me, and not knowing what was going on. I was so tired.

"Okay, okay. Fran's a doctor, blah blah blah, has been doing research into aging and longevity and DNA and other stuff I just don't understand but apparently you can do things to your own DNA now? With like, mail order kits even if you aren't a doctor? And she did it to herself first and can see a change anyway, under a microscope, it like. Self edits once introduced to the bloodstream. No, self multiplies. Edits the rest of the DNA. But of course we don't know if she fixed us until we know if she fixed us. But that's why Betty was suddenly so friendly, if you wondered. Did you wonder?"

"That's amazing," I said. It didn't even seem real, that maybe Fran fixed us. Maybe we wouldn't die in our forties anymore just because. But... "But what's that got to do with Silvernail?"

"Oh well, we were talking about that at the one house, after you got shot, and when Fran was giving us our kitchen table inoculations and then Everett said something like 'a few years ago, people figured out that they could actually store computer viruses in DNA and it would corrupt the systems of whatever was analyzing it' and so I guess ultimately he's the one to blame for my idea of letting myself get kidnapped, so let's keep that in mind when we're pointing fingers, but so I asked him how long it would take him to whip something up like that and of course the fucker already *had* because that's what people like that are like and so against medical advice, I had Fran add that as well."

"Why would she—"

"Because she knew I was going to do it anyway so it might as well be with supervision. It's like you've never met me sometimes, I swear to god."

"Morgan," Luke rumbled, and she glanced at him.

"So anyway, Allie, we're the same blood type and while you got some emergency universal donor blood for your first transfusion that the Wards had kicking around for just such an occasion, for your second transfusion, it was mine. After both these other things happened."

"Oh." I still sat at the table, just stunned. Morgan laughed.

"Anyway I forgot but I'm sure Everett didn't, so he's probably been keeping tabs. Fuck, this could be good news."

"It also probably means that Allie needs another blood transfusion," Joe said.

"Oh yeah, probably," Morgan said, but she didn't sound too concerned. "Got any in the fridge, Luke?"

"Did it look like I did?"

"I didn't move the mustard," she said, laughing again. "Okay well I'm gonna eat, I'm starving."

"I'll just give Everett a call," Luke said. "For our peace of mind."

I was the only one who laughed.

# Chapter Eighteen

My mind thought I wasn't hungry but my body disagreed, and even though what Morgan bought us were sandwiches bigger than I'd ever seen meant for a single person to consume, I ate my whole thing. And a bunch of the fried green beans, even though I couldn't decide if I actually liked them or not. I was too tired again already to think much about it, and too terrified at the same time about Rachel, about Silvernail, about everything. And being in Luke's house wasn't helping me much, no matter how little he was here, no matter how much he'd been trying to be good to us just lately, despite our early impressions. My early impressions. Morgan had always liked what she saw, I guess. He didn't even come out to the parking lot to fight, that first meeting, and I still didn't know why. Bill told him not to, I guessed. Maybe Bill thought, knew, he'd take something too far. That always seemed like the risk, with a Luke. With a Morgan. A Hunter.

Morgan's phone rang right as I nodded off at the table, and it scared me so bad that I knocked my chair over but somehow didn't fall on the floor myself.

"Hunter, fucking finally," she said, frowning at me. "What's going on? How—" She stopped and listened, and we all listened, but I couldn't hear Hunter. I couldn't tell if Luke or Joe could hear. Morgan's face didn't really change, her posture didn't change, nothing. "You tell her—" her voice broke off, and I think it surprised even her, and the phone creaked a very soft protest in her hand. "Yeah, I know. I *know*. You too." The call ended and she delicately set the phone in front of her on the kitchen table.

Joe picked up my chair, startling me.

"What did Hunter say?" I asked when it seemed like Morgan was just going to sit there and not say anything. Morgan was sitting too still. Morgan never sat still like that.

"Fran is doing what she can," Morgan said, in a very level tone, that only scared me more. "Fran and some Ward medics."

"But they..." I started, but didn't know where to go

"Nope." She pushed back slowly from the table. "Nothing is better but nothing is worse and that's where we are with that."

"Well that's—"

"Save it, Joe," she said, and the danger in her voice was a physical feeling.

"Well, I guess you need to choose if you want to go for a run or if you want to hit something," Luke said in the taut silence. "I've got both a heavy bag and a speed bag in the basement, or there's a piece of woods not far from here. The kids need sleep, they're at their limit, and we're here until at least tomorrow, probably the day after."

"*You're* at your limit," she said, curling her lip a little

"And so are you, but sometimes there's nothing else for it," he said, shrugging. "And I think I'm going to go for that run even if you don't. I've been up long enough that I'm too wired." Besides that he'd left Everett a voicemail and also hadn't heard back yet.

He headed for the back door, out of the kitchen, and I watched Morgan get mad about that too before she followed him. There was a lot more air in the room without those two in it.

"He wasn't wrong, I'm asleep on my feet," Joe said. I realized I was still standing next to the table where I'd startled awake. "I think Morgan has sleep clothes in that bag, if you want to get changed."

"Yeah, sleeping in jeans isn't great," I said.

"Sleeping in jeans, in the back of a truck, not sleeping at all," Joe said, and I laughed.

"We'll write a new Dr. Seuss book except just for werewolf families in crisis."

"It's a great idea," he said. "The kind of thing normal people won't realize, but wolves will know."

I rummaged in the clothes bag and did find sleep clothes, and got changed in Luke's bathroom, which was both as clean and abandoned feeling as the rest of the house. He even had little toothpastes, not a big one, and I spent too long wondering about that. Did toothpaste actually go bad, if a big one was opened and then left alone for a few weeks or months? The strip of my hair that Hunter dyed kept startling me in the mirror.

I ran into Joe in the hallway. I must've taken long enough to worry him. "Sorry," I said.

"No, it's okay. I didn't want you to come out alone, and not know where to go." It was a small enough house that it would've been okay, I thought. It was very thoughtful of him, I thought.

"I'm about ready to just fall over."

"Well, the rooms are made up, so you can fall over right there." I followed Joe into one of the most basic of guest bedrooms: bed, bedside table, dresser. The closet wasn't empty as I expected; the door was partway open, and suits hung on the rail there. Shoe boxes were on the floor, and I guessed they were probably shiny dress shoes, waiting for occasions.

He turned to go and I said "Wait," without meaning to, or without knowing what I was going to say next. But he didn't make me say it.

"It's okay," he said. "I'll get changed and be back."

"Thank you," I said. I sat on the bed, feeling nervous, shaky, more exhausted than I ever had in my life. Feeling guilty, but there wasn't anything to be guilty about. There wasn't anything wrong with feeling bad, after what happened, and what happened wasn't my fault. There wasn't anything wrong with wanting and needing comfort. There wasn't anything wrong with just sleeping in the same bed as somebody.

I didn't remember getting under blankets, or Joe coming to lay down, but I woke up when he got up in the darkness. "Getting a drink," he said quietly. I must have made a noise, or maybe asked something. I relaxed back into almost-sleep, but some part of my brain had sharpened, and I listened to him move through the house. Luke was in the kitchen, I thought. Joe had to know that. I was thinking of Luke like the big bad wolf in his own house and that wasn't very generous of my spirit.

I didn't hear what Joe said, but I heard Luke say "Don't worry about it." and Joe ran the tap and then I heard Luke say "You're doing good. I'm proud of you."

Joe made a noise like a laugh, except it was a torn, hurt little sound. "Are you kidding me?"

"No." The silence spun out long enough that I wondered if I was actually still asleep, actually dreaming. Then Luke sighed. "I treated you badly, and I'm sorry."

"You're *sorry*?" Joe said, too loud, and I didn't know I'd been aware of Morgan's sleep breathing until it stopped. It was weird that she was asleep but Luke wasn't. Morgan didn't sleep good.

"Yeah. I'm sorry." I prayed Morgan wasn't going to get up and butt in, but I didn't hear her doing that. Yet.

"Well." Joe was fumbling, maybe furious, maybe heartbroken. "I'm glad you're sorry. Because between you and Dad…"

Luke actually waited a long time for him to keep going. "Yeah, I know." A chair scraped on the floor. "I can't change his mind, just mine."

"I don't expect him to change his mind." A longer pause. He didn't expect either of them to change their minds. "Why now?"

"I don't know. Because of how you've handled yourself on these ops. Because I realize now how shitty it all is. Because I want to be a better dad than that, when the time comes."

A noise that confused me, that I realized a second later was a punch. "Fuck. Ow, fuck."

"Yeah, there's a reason not to punch people in the face," Luke said wryly, rattling ice in the freezer.

"I'm—"

"No, I deserved that. Worse. But at least that. At least you didn't go for the nose." More chairs scraping. "Here."

I wished I'd seen this reconciliation, or this start of one, and I was glad they'd had it alone, even if Morgan and I both definitely heard it. I didn't know how I was going to pretend that I hadn't, but I was going to try. My anxious mind was trying to find a way to gnaw on that when I fell asleep again.

I woke up again when Joe set a bottle of water on the nightstand by me. I was cold, but sweaty at the same time, shaking again. Maybe the shaking woke me up. I should send him to sleep someplace else. "Thanks," I mumbled. Did I dream all of that? Did he and Luke have that conversation in the kitchen or no? I could hear Morgan talking, I thought. Feel the baritone of Luke's answers. "Are you okay?" I asked, or tried to ask.

"Shh, yes," he said, pulling the blanket up over my shoulder. "Just go back to sleep." That was all I needed to be gone again.

I didn't sleep as soundly this time, though, and my dreams were full of lights. Party lights, ambulance lights, lab lights, street lights, headlights. Hot asphalt and burned rubber and blood and screaming and I screamed myself awake, finding my voice and screaming the way I couldn't ever before.

"Allie, wake up." Morgan was shaking me, Morgan had been shaking me, but it didn't work until it did. "Allie fucking *stop*." I took a breath, I thought maybe to scream again, and she hauled off and slapped me full in the face, rocking my head back.

"Jesus," Luke said, but maybe it was the right decision, because I was awake and not screaming anymore. Poor Joe looked very bewildered and I'm sure everybody's ears were ringing. We were all in that one room, listening to me pant.

"I'm sorry," I said. "I'm sorry I just..." But I couldn't even describe it. And none of them asked me, I realized. Nobody asked me what any of it was like. What happened. Did I want to talk about it anyway? Was I capable? I didn't really think so.

Morgan huffed out a breath and stood back, her hands on her hips. "Well that was invigorating." I put my hand to my cheek, where it stung.

"I'm sorry," I said again.

"It's okay," Joe said, because nobody else was. "We keep just dragging you around places and it isn't fair. You need time."

"Sometimes there isn't time," Morgan snapped.

"What about after, Morgan?" I asked.

"What?"

"There's always an after." She blinked at me.

"Is there?"

• • • •

I TOOK A SHOWER, AND it was disorienting to use Luke's shampoo and soap, but felt good to stand under the water. I probably took too long of a shower, but nobody banged on the door to yell at me. I toweled off and got dressed in clothes that Morgan gave me, which might have been hers, I didn't know. At least I knew why my shoulder felt so much better, even though I'd fallen on it in the escape. Two weeks. I wiped the steam off the mirror and tried to look at the stitches in my neck, but couldn't really see. They didn't shave my head, there was that. They had me longer than they did the aunts, but didn't shave my head.

I looked at my arms, needle pricks in them, bruises blooming in bouquets at each spot. Then I sat on the bathroom floor with my back against the tub, my hands over my mouth so that if I made any noise in spite of myself it would be quieter, and cried some more. God this was terrible. God this was hard.

Somebody banged out the front door and I thought oh what now, pausing in my self-pity to listen. The truck tailgate slammed, and the front door opened and closed again, and Luke said, "Here, do something with this," in what I was thinking of as his 'fed up but still trying to be decent' voice.

"Oh, fuck you," Morgan said, but automatically, without an edge to it. Then I heard the latches on a hard guitar case. "This one's Allie's." Luke kind of wordlessly grumbled and she said, "Fine, fine."

I got my breathing under control and ran the water cold, washed my face again, as I listened to Morgan thumb through the strings and adjust the tuning. She played a few chords, but didn't really settle into anything by the time I came out of the bathroom. She looked at me and there wasn't anything for the hurt and anger in her eyes.

I stopped at the end of the hall, where the door between the kitchen and living room were, and Luke looked at me from where he stood in front of the open fridge.

"How do you like your eggs?" he asked.

"You're cooking us eggs?" I asked, feeling no less off balance than when I woke up screaming.

"If you want them," he said, shrugging.

"Scrambled," I said. I liked them over easy too, but I didn't want to ask for too much. I also didn't know when he might have made eggs appear in the fridge, from what it seemed like last night, it was full of beer and mustard. Maybe he went and got them from his neighbor. Maybe he just went to the store. Maybe it didn't matter and I was focusing on things that didn't matter so that I didn't have to think about everything that was wrong and big and scary. Joe edged past me into the bathroom, and I sat on the opposite end of the couch from Morgan.

What a weird domestic scene, I thought, as Luke fried eggs and the shower ran and Morgan strummed on the guitar.

"Is that Rooster?" Luke asked after a minute.

She stopped. "Yeah."

"No, keep going."

She sighed like she was mad, but she did. "Did you watch the livestream?"

"I did, yeah," he said. "Hunter did your makeup?"

"Was it that obvious?"

"It was just the first time I'd seen you wearing any." The toaster popped. "That's you, Allie."

I didn't know how to just talk to Luke, I realized. Or almost anybody, I guessed. I felt like I had to have a reason to say something, or I'd get in trouble somehow. I went to the kitchen, chewing on that thought. My eggs were on a plate next to the toaster, fresh stick of butter in the butter dish. "Thank you," I said.

"You're welcome," he said. "You're always so damn polite."

"Sorry." He laughed, and Morgan stopped playing.

"I didn't mean it was a bad thing." He pointed at the drawer in front of me, and I opened it to find the silverware. "Morgan, eggs?"

"Over easy." She started playing again as I scraped butter on my toast and wondered if I should eat at the table or go back to the couch. Table, probably, even though it kept me in the room with Luke. She was playing a Howling song, one that was normally fast, but slow. It made me think of the day she bought the guitars, with the sun shining, and Dio panting happily in the back seat.

Luke didn't have a dog, I realized, or didn't have a dog here. I almost asked about that, and then considered the melancholy of hearing that he'd once had a dog here and why he didn't anymore, and I took my plate to the table without asking. I couldn't ask him that. I heard Morgan's phone buzz and I stopped with the fork halfway to my mouth, and she let the last chord ring out as she checked it and I thought answered, but she didn't say anything. I saw the way Luke reacted to that noise, just a little, tensing up and then relaxing, still facing the stove, and I thought that he never had a dog. In his mind, I thought, Luke had always been at war.

Joe came and sat across from me as Luke plated up Morgan's eggs and toast and put them on the table. He didn't say anything, and she kept playing for a second. I knew, but Luke didn't know, that she was finishing the song, and I watched him pick up the next egg. Hold it. "Joe?"

Joe looked at me. Oh good, he thought this was weird too. "However you're having them," he said.

Luke nodded and cracked eggs into the pan and Morgan finished the last verse and set the guitar in the case, stomped out to the kitchen. Maybe she was doing that to cover her limp. "How long are we gonna be here for?" she asked, dropping into her seat. "Because I need to go to—"

"I know you do," Luke said.

"Well okay then, we're going right?"

"No."

"What the fuck do you mean, no."

"The last thing we need right now is for any of us to go off half-cocked and to draw even more attention. We need to let the medics and your sister do their work, and we need to see if Everett's virus thing works, and when that comes together we can go. Unless Bill sends us somewhere else in the meanwhile." I wondered if we were ever going to hear him call Bill 'Dad.'

"I'm not one of your soldiers, Luke," Morgan said, and when he turned around, her smile was the calm, flashing knife blade kind not the brash grin, not the fuck you, I dare you to stop me smile. Morgan was her most dangerous when she was quiet and focused, and she'd gotten all the loud out for now.

And Luke didn't take the bait.

"Nobody's confused about that," he said.

She stood up, knocking her chair back but not over, jostling the table. "Then what is the *problem* here? Let's go."

He turned away to get plates down, and I saw the effort that it took for him, to turn his back on Morgan when she was like this. "Joe and I aren't going anywhere. I guess if you and Allie are leaving, you'll just need to figure it out for yourselves."

"Isn't that just how it always is? Me and Allie figuring it out for ourselves?"

"Apparently it is. So you'll be comfortable." He set a plate in front of Joe, sat down with his food, leaving Morgan standing over the table, flexing her fists.

"That's it?" she asked.

He put his elbows on the table, looked up at her. "I don't know what else you want from me, Morgan."

"My mother is…is *hurt* and you're not letting me go wherever it is the medics are working to be with her so I maybe need a little more than 'yeah I guess you could leave but you're on your own again, good luck with that.' You get that, right?"

He nodded, keeping his breathing even. "Yeah. Yeah, I get that." She was trying so hard to fight with him, and he was trying so hard to keep level and I didn't realize I was holding my breath until Joe kicked me under the table and I gasped and then coughed. Morgan cut her eyes to me with such a furious, disdainful look that I shrank away from her.

"Allie? I could use some backup here?"

"I know," I said. "I hate not being there too."

"I'm not being cruel to you on purpose," Luke said. "We're trying to do damage control here and prevent other injury and loss. We just gave Silvernail the biggest push we ever have, and need to—"

"Go to ground, we always need to *fucking* go to ground." I thought for a second Morgan was going to flip the table for the sake of it. That was what Rachel said the day we went to get the wolf. Go to ground. "We need to burn it all down."

"We can't burn it all down or we wouldn't be doing this stupid shit," Luke snapped.

"The last thing they will expect us to do right now is hit them again," Morgan said. "We get Everett in on this, we track down one of theirs. One of their little party girls, or that guy in the suit. We don't let up the pressure."

"Maybe we should," I said slowly. Joe looked at me like his eyes might fall out. I couldn't look at Luke. "They don't care. We aren't people, we're subjects, we're things. Our behavior doesn't matter, really, our lives don't matter. If *they* lost somebody, it'll matter to them. And that Silvernail, the one I was in the room with...he isn't going to stop." I could still smell his anger, his outrage, and I shivered. "The man in the suit. He's the one who likes going loaded with silver so much. He's the one who likes hurting us."

"W-we don't actually want to do that," Joe said and I swung my head around at him fast enough my neck cracked. If I was a wolf my hackles would be up.

"Why not? What have you lost? What happened to *you*?" I could smell Morgan's satisfaction, her approval.

Joe put his hands up. "I...nothing. But you'll lose more of *yourself* than you want to, if you kill one of theirs, like that. That isn't you, Allie, you aren't like that."

"Yeah? What am I like?" Never mind the fact that I was scrubbing tears off my face with the sleeve of my shirt, which wasn't even my shirt, was another one of somebody's t-shirts washed and worn soft. But my brief anger was circling into misery again, into stomach twisting anxiety.

"What he means is I'm the one like that," Morgan said, voice sharp and quiet again. "Isn't that what you mean, Joe."

"I, um." Joe looked from me to Morgan, calculating, and shrugged. "I guess, yeah, it might be what I mean." He glanced at Luke briefly, for support or appeal, I couldn't say. Luke had the look on his face that he did the first time we walked into that back room at the Bear's Den.

"It's fine, Joe, I know who I am. Allie's still figuring it out I guess." She sat down at the table again, hitched her chair in. "So what then? If we don't kill them, what? We don't want to start with this hostage bullshit."

"We aren't starting with any of this bullshit," Luke said. Morgan started to growl again and he held up a hand. "Eat your fucking breakfast, and I'll call Bill to get cleared to get you to Rachel. Is that good enough?"

"It's what I was asking for," she said, with a little less crackle.

# Chapter Nineteen

Morgan kept looking at her phone, cracking her knuckles, shifting her weight this way and that, leaning forward to change the radio. Finally Luke pulled over and made her and Joe switch so she was in the front seat. "So you don't kill us all in a wreck," he said. "I'm not ruling out other methods of course."

"Luke, that's the nicest thing you've ever said to me," she said, smiling sweetly, teeth bared just a little too long.

"See I'm an okay guy once you get to know me," he said, with no change to his deadpan expression. I laughed, and he looked at me, obviously surprised.

"You made us eggs," I said, as if that explained anything.

We kept driving. Nobody said where we were going. I didn't pay attention to any of the signs. I didn't know what I didn't know, and if I got grabbed again, if I didn't know something I couldn't tell it. I didn't know if I was being smart or profoundly stupid.

Morgan stretched in her seat, still jumpy, still an angry jangly bundle of wanting to fight, wanting to hurt something. But she was getting what she wanted, and that helped as much as it could.

About three hours in, her phone rang, and she jerked it to her ear. "Tell me."

There was a pause, not enough that Morgan got any more amped up than she already was, but a good three heartbeats, and then Hunter said "Honey, I'm so sorry, she's gone."

"FUCK," Morgan yelled, and she almost threw her phone, went through the motion but kept it in her hand. She punched the dashboard and Luke reached over and caught her hand awkwardly when she racked back to do it again, swerving the truck a little. "Fuck," she said again, quieter. Hunter was still talking, I could hear Hunter talking, but not what she said, over the heartbeat in my ears and Morgan, and then Morgan put the phone to her ear again. "You were with her?" She listened then nodded like Hunter could hear her. "Okay. Okay. Yes. Okay. Thank you. We're...fuck it I don't know where we are. Fuck." She hung up, threw the phone on the dash, put her face in her hands.

She wasn't crying. She was very still, breathing very slowly, like she was concentrating on every single one, in and out and in and out. Luke drove, tightening and loosening his hands on the steering wheel, looking over at Morgan occasionally, checking the mirrors more frequently.

Rachel was gone.

I probably knew it from the moment I heard her cry out, from the moment I saw her there on the road. But I prayed anyway. For all the good it ever did.

When we found out that Dulcie was dead, we couldn't stop to think about it. We still had to get Rachel on her feet, get ourselves out of that Silvernail facility. Here, though. Now, though. We were just in this truck, still driving towards a hope we didn't have anymore.

I leaned over and forward, put my hand on Morgan's shoulder. She gave a shrugging wiggle to shake me off and I squeezed instead. She dropped her hands, turned around to glare at me. I felt strangely frozen, outside of things, like I'd put myself in a box in order to keep going. I wished I'd learned this trick earlier. Maybe it was an accident, and I'd never be able to do it again. But her glare didn't scare me, for once. "Have Hunter come meet us," I said. "Luke, pick a place for us to be. Not a motel, away from people." Like Morgan was an explosive, I thought. Like she had to be handled. But she kind of was.

"Roger that," he said. Morgan took a big heaving breath like she was going to yell, or cry, or anything, but instead she turned back around and stretched for her phone. Leaned forward how I was, I could see her clearing alerts first, one by one, hesitating over the last one, cocking her head a little like there was a thought she couldn't quite grasp. Then she sent a text, got an immediate response.

"Where?" she asked in a leaden tone.

"I'm thinking, hold on." He seemed to catch Joe's eyes in the rearview for a minute. "Camp Bravo. Do you remember how to get there or—"

"I fucking remember," she snapped. She typed for a long time, got a bunch of buzzes in response, huffed again. Luke offered her a pack of cigarettes, and she took one, taking the plastic lighter they'd been using. It took her two tries to light it.

This was my best idea, and I hoped it wasn't an awful one, but I couldn't see putting Morgan in a location with a bunch of Wards, and her golden child doctor sister, and I was glad that Luke caught on to that as easily as he did. Maybe I was robbing Fran of some comfort, doing this, but I didn't think so.

Morgan just sat staring straight out the front windshield, alternating between balling her fists up and gripping her knees, until her knuckles turned white and the scars and fresh scabs across them stood out stark.

At some point on the drive, as we left the highway and wound to Camp Bravo on local roads, Joe reached over and took my hand. I looked at him and he gave it a gentle squeeze; he wasn't going to say he was sorry, and I wasn't going to say I was okay. I squeezed his hand back, and we sat that way the rest of the ride.

None of us had said it, that Rachel was dead. That Rachel died. We didn't need to say it, we all heard Hunter. Even though that wasn't exactly what Hunter said.

We got to Camp Bravo and Luke got out of the truck and did a sweep in one direction, and Joe went in the other, while I watched them in confusion and Morgan lit another cigarette. "For all their wargames, they still couldn't..." she said, but just kind of shook her head and didn't finish the thought. I listened to them move over the uneven ground, imagining how different but the same it would be in the summer, versus in the fall when we were here last. No fallen leaves to crunch on, everything damp and green and the dew just starting to get cooked off it by the hot sun. Thought about how different it was then, with all the Wards here, with Sela here, freshly rescued. Back when we thought everybody was still alive. Back when everybody was still alive.

Tires crunched on the gravel drive, bringing Luke back immediately, but Morgan turned slowly, dropping her cigarette and dragging her toe over it. She knew it was Hunter, and because she knew, I knew. Who else would drive a brand new convertible Land Rover up here?

Hunter jammed her car into park and jumped out, and she didn't even take her keys or close the door, she just hugged

Morgan, who struggled against her for a minute and then accepted the embrace, her face pressed against Hunter's shoulder.

It felt like it was intruding to watch, and I turned away to see Joe come from around the back of the cabin. He looked at Hunter and Morgan, and looked at Luke, who shrugged. If Rachel was the way to get under Morgan's skin, then Hunter knew the way to her heart, and I loved her for it. Morgan wasn't crying, wasn't suddenly displaying an outpouring of grief, but I couldn't expect that. It just wasn't her. She was furious, and she was hurting so bad it was like the wound was physical.

In the aftermath of when Dulcie died, Morgan was also dealing with recovering from being shot, and the satisfaction and relief of rescuing Rachel, and Sela. There was payoff. She still had Rachel. Now, what she had was me, and I'd been the problem all along, hadn't I?

I went up on the porch with Luke and Joe, followed them inside. Joe walked around and opened a couple of windows, and Luke went upstairs, maybe still on his guard but being casual about it. I didn't hear anything, didn't smell anything. As far as I could tell, nobody had been here since we all left last fall. Eventually, Luke seemed to come to that same conclusion, and came back down to the main room. He looked out the screen door; Morgan and Hunter were in the same spot, maybe spun in place a little like they were slow dancing, and I could hear the murmur of Hunter's voice, but not her words. That was just for Morgan.

"I'm surprised every time I see that streak in your hair," Joe said with a hesitant smile.

"Me too," I said. If things were different, I thought, he would've reached over to touch it. Maybe tuck that lock of hair behind my ear. "I catch a glimpse in the mirror, or out of the corner of my eye, and think something is on me. A big moth or something."

"Not your idea, then."

"No, Hunter's. No, I never did anything with my hair. I've always kept it long, even." Why was I talking about my hair? Rachel was dead.

"So it was your first time dying your hair, and you just let Hunter do it randomly in a hotel room?" Joe asked. I looked at him. He was doing this on purpose, trying to distract me, get me in an okay place to settle.

"Well she'd done Morgan's hair and had some left over and they're both forces of nature, so. Yeah, that's exactly what happened."

Luke half laughed. "Forces of nature. You've got that right."

Out front, Hunter's car turned off and the door slammed, and then they came up on the porch and inside. Morgan was still red eyed and hurt and furious. Hunter looked more watchful and serious than I'd seen her before. She surprised me by catching me up in a sudden hug; she was here for Morgan, what was she comforting me for?

"Allie, what a nightmare," she said. "Just all of it." She let me go, and stepped back. "We're just going to have some time and not have anything *scheduled* or *on the docket* and let other people sort things out for once, okay? Okay. You hear me, Luke Ward?" She pointed accusingly.

"Okay," he said, putting his hands up. "I can't promise things won't get put on my docket."

"Good enough. And I don't think they will," she said. "Just a suspicion I have."

"If you say so," Luke said. He already looked antsy, at the prospect of nothing to do. So did Morgan, but she hadn't ever in my time knowing her stopped looking as though she wanted to be in constant motion.

"I *do* say so, you people need to learn how to give yourself space and time after a trauma." Hunter gave a little huff, and I wouldn't have been surprised if she stamped her foot. "Anyway, there's groceries in the back of my car. And Morgan's electric guitar and pedalboard and mini amp but I don't think we're at that stage right now?"

"No," Morgan said. She was standing in front of the fireplace, staring up at the moose head. Joe went out to Hunter's car.

"You're welcome. Vinnie was very happy to see me and is always utterly confused and accepting of what you do anyway. A true gem."

"He's one of a kind, that Vinnie. He's gonna make a special lady very happy one of these days."

"Morgan."

"I don't know what you want me to do, Hunter. What's the right thing for me to be doing? There isn't any right thing."

Joe came back on the porch and Luke went and got the door for him, took one of the bags and carried it through to the kitchen. I felt like I should do something, but I also didn't want to distract from Morgan. Or draw her attention and anger.

"Allie, go help the menfolk," Hunter said, rescuing me. "They simply can't be trusted."

I fled to the kitchen, got there as Luke was saying "She bought a blender?" in the most confused voice I'd ever heard from him.

"Hunter is very thorough," I said, like that was an answer. Joe got it, but Luke blinked at me. "Morgan likes milkshakes."

"We're going for a run," Hunter called, as the door banged shut behind them. It was funny that us and the Wards and the Coutards called it that; maybe all wolves called it that. Though I could also imagine Hunter actually going for a run, in exercise clothes, hair in a ponytail, listening to music on earbuds. Maybe Howling; Morgan's music might make good exercise music.

"We probably shouldn't..." I said, trailing off. I was going to say that we probably shouldn't just let them go off, but really, we probably shouldn't, or couldn't, stop them. I didn't think Hunter was going to let Morgan do anything big and reckless right now. I hoped.

Luke shrugged, maybe having the same thoughts. "It's just in God's hands I guess," he said in a dry voice, and I couldn't figure out how serious or how funny he was trying to be.

• • • •

HUNTER'S GROCERIES did not include liquor or beer. Morgan started to ramp up about that when they got back, but Hunter wheedled her away from the kitchen, then got her smoothed out and sat on the porch steps while they were still breathing hard. She set out a little boom box that played cassettes and CDs, popped in one of Morgan's car tapes and then took her sweet time combing out Morgan's hair and then braiding it, black-white black-white like album cover candy canes. They smelled like moss and pine needles and creek, and I wondered how far they ran.

Hunter's groceries did include steaks, and potato salad, and ears of corn, and while they were gone, Luke got the grill fired up and cleaned, so it couldn't have been too far, or too long. Maybe they should've gone longer, honestly, though we all knew by now what it took to actually exhaust Morgan, and it was a lot. But Hunter had that way about her, of making things seem appealing, and like good and nice ideas, and when she turned to me and said "Okay, let me do your hair now too" I went and sat on the steps in front of her, next to Morgan. It was easy to forget how nice it felt, to have somebody comb your hair and braid it for you.

I heard Luke answer his phone out back, over the sizzles of the grill, and I tried not to listen because I wasn't sure what I could take anymore. I tried to concentrate on the music on the tape, or on the creek that was just down the driveway, shallow water running across rocks, but then I heard him say "Jesus fucking Christ, good news for once?" and Morgan was on her feet and rounding the cabin to be in on it. I started to get up too, and Hunter put her hands on my shoulders, gentle but firm.

"It's okay, we'll find out soon enough," she said. I slumped a little with relief, and she kept combing. "Who did your stitches?"

"Luke."

"That makes sense. They look too good for Morgan to have tried."

"She didn't care," I said, trying not to sound bitter about it. It was my own fault that Morgan had to hurt me, it wasn't fair to be mad at her for it. Not with everything.

"No, I suppose she wouldn't," Hunter said, sectioning my braids.

"Don't say anything to her," I said. Maybe she heard us anyway, but maybe she was distracted enough by Luke and the phone.

"I won't, but you're going to have to figure yourselves out eventually," she said, snapping the elastic on my braid end as Morgan yelled for us from out back. "Milady summons us."

"The whole mountain knows," I said. I almost couldn't believe that anybody had good news. Good news for who? How good?

The grill was smoking wildly out back, the steaks forgotten, Luke still on the phone and Joe and Morgan with their heads near his, because why use speakerphone when you're werewolves. I picked up the tongs and got the steaks onto the waiting platter; they were probably fine, but I couldn't sort out Everett's voice from the hissing and spitting. Luke hung up, and we all kind of stood around looking at each other.

"Okay, now one of you tell the rest of the class," Hunter said, smiling.

"Silvernail's done," Morgan said. "The DNA thing worked, their systems are eating themselves."

"But that's just the computers," I said. I saw that man's face. He wasn't going to give up because he didn't have computers anymore.

"Yeah, but the whole world is computers now. Their money is in the computers. All of their data, all of their documentation, except whatever was already printed out. We saw how much they printed out, the first time. Did you see any printouts when you were there?"

"No," I said, too stunned to be tripped up by the question. When I was there. At the clinic, when Hunter and I pretended to do an interview? No printouts. When they had me chained to a bed? No printouts. "That can't be it, it isn't that simple. That man—"

"Allie this is a *win*!" Morgan said, too loud. Mad at me, impatient, what else was new. Hunter put a hand on her arm, and she shook her off.

"Well okay tell her the rest," Luke said. "It isn't just that the techs know their infrastructure is crumbling. Silvernail called Rachel's phone."

"He what?"

"He called Rachel's phone. And he offered a ceasefire."

"We can't trust that," I said. I felt crazy, like I was the only one who didn't see how anything was solved. Nothing was fixed.

"Well it's not like we can get anything on paper, but Bill is tentatively hopeful."

"He called Rachel's phone and made a deal with *Bill*?" Now I was getting mad, too, and I didn't know if that made any sense.

"No, he made a deal with Fran," Morgan said.

"I wish..." I wish I'd just killed him, I couldn't make myself say. We were his pet project, pun intended, and what kind of corporation was going to keep going with what he'd been doing, once they found out? Maybe I'd scared him enough. Maybe it was good enough.

"Any one of these things, and we wouldn't be so happy about this," Joe said. He looked a little stunned too. "But all of them together, and they need to figure out how to even keep existing. Everett can explain this better, we're not doing a good job I don't think. Like, I know you understand what we're saying it's just—"

"It's just a lot," I said. "It just seems too good to be true. Like there's going to be something else."

"There's always something else," Luke said, but I felt like maybe he actually understood me. "Just take the win."

"See, now we *do* need beer," Morgan said to Hunter, who laughed ruefully.

"Or champagne."

"Isn't there a beer that's the champagne of beers? We can go get that."

Hunter scrunched her face up. "No, thank you."

"I really can't fucking believe this. Okay so I'm with you on it a little, Allie. But stop being such a killjoy, I mean it."

"I'll try," I said. Maybe it was true. Or maybe it was just good enough for now, and sometimes, that's all we can hope for.

# Chapter Twenty

We ate the steaks and Luke didn't let anybody go and buy beer. We weren't really on a mission anymore, I thought. We didn't really have an 'op' anymore, but it was hard to let go and just let Morgan and Hunter go shopping on the assumption that they would ever come back. And maybe it wouldn't matter, if they didn't. But instead Luke did the next best thing, in Morgan's eyes, or maybe even better, which was reveal the location of the hidden liquor cabinet.

"Oh fuck yes, time for mudslides," Morgan said, taking an armful of bottles to the kitchen. "We don't have chocolate syrup, but we'll cope."

"I actually think there is a new bottle in one of the cabinets," Joe said, following her.

"None of us *like* chocolate," I said, always trailing behind. I didn't know what a mudslide was either, but I wasn't going to ask.

"It's just a little, for effect," Morgan said. "*Garnish*"

"A contrast to the sweet," Hunter agreed. They were building to the same energy as in the hotel room prior to the Howling livestream, and I knew better than to get in the way of that as they fired up the blender and mixed the drinks and passed them around. I knew better than to try and make sense of Morgan's mood, which was a dark one, we could all smell that on her, but she also wasn't going to let this opportunity pass us by. I just felt like we were walking that knife's edge again, and who knew which side any of us were going to come down on.

Too much happened in too short a time, and it needed more time to sink in. Definitely for me, absolutely for Morgan, but I wasn't going to say anything like that to her. I was just going to try to stay out of her way.

It was weird being at a Ward camp with this few people, and last time we were here, Morgan and I just slept on couches. Hoyt deployed, I remember him saying. I wonder where Zeb was, where he lived. If he deployed too. After I drank part of my mudslide, I gave the rest to Morgan and stumbled off up to the room I remembered them having Sela in. They gave her saline IVs, I remembered. I wasn't drinking enough water, I thought. Somebody said I wasn't just going to walk this off; I probably shouldn't have had *any* mudslide.

I slept but not soundly; I felt like I heard everybody else moving around the cabin. Having more drinks, or putting away food, or finding a bedroom. I thought that maybe Joe paused in my doorway, but he didn't come in, maybe because I already seemed to be sleeping. Maybe because I hadn't asked. Or maybe I dreamed all of it.

It was still full dark when I jerked awake and slapped Morgan's hand as she reached down to shake me, before I realized it was her. "Shh, stop it, wake up. It's me."

I sat up. "What is it? Are you okay?"

"No I'm not okay but that isn't why I'm waking you up." She still smelled like the woods, but also like the grillsmoke and mudslides and Hunter.

"Oh." Squeezed my eyes shut, opened them again.

"I'd tell you to get dressed, but I don't think you got changed. Come on, we're leaving."

"We're leaving? Where are we going? Did you tell Luke?"

"Why would I tell Luke? And it's a surprise. For you."

"For *me*?" I couldn't begin to imagine what Morgan would decide to surprise me with in the middle of the night after her mother died. Or why. She shushed me again, but I'd probably already made enough noise to wake up everybody who wasn't me and Morgan and Hunter, I didn't know why she kept shushing me.

"Okay maybe it's a little bit for me too but come on. You can sleep again in the car, but it's only like, an hour and a half."

I thought for a second about what it would be like to tell her no, and to stay. But what would that get me? Why would I stay with Joe and Luke, and what would that end up as, now that we weren't pushing back against Silvernail anymore?

Joe would probably go back to Bill's and Luke would go wherever it was he went that wasn't his house and I didn't belong there with them either. No matter how well Joe and I were getting along, how very slowly we were getting to know and like each other. Where would I go, if it wasn't with Morgan? I didn't have anywhere to be. "Okay."

"Meet us outside in a few." Even though I watched her leave the room, I hardly heard her, she was that quiet. I got up slowly, self-consciously, even though nobody was in the room watching me. I snuck out of a house of werewolves when I was very impaired on painkillers after being shot with silver; I was in much better shape now, right? Maybe the painkillers helped make me brave, before. The cabin wasn't very creaky, though, and once I decided I'd put my boots on in Hunter's car, I didn't really have anything else to worry about. I wished I had the time to leave a note for Joe, but I didn't think Morgan would let me take that long before coming back to find me. I wished

I had a phone so I could text him, but I hadn't yet replaced the one I lost to Silvernail.

I crept down the stairs and across the great room, under the moose head's watchful eye, eased the door open and then shut again behind me, and made it to Hunter's vehicle without raising an alarm or shaking myself anxiously apart. I got in the back seat and buckled in and Hunter looked at me, and looked at Morgan, and said, "Are you sure?"

"I'm sure."

Hunter shrugged and put it in gear and we drove away. I didn't notice, before, that her engine itself made hardly any noise. Convertible *and* electric, or at least hybrid. I didn't know why I was so focused on that; maybe I thought we'd somehow make enough noise, and Luke would stop us. I had no reason to want Luke to stop us, other than that I was scared about Morgan's surprise.

Not too scared to fall back asleep, though. I did that just fine, waking up when we stopped at a convenience store and Morgan put a giant bottle of water in my hands and told me to drink. "We're almost there," she added.

"Will you tell me what the surprise is now?" I asked fuzzily.

"Drink some of that first." She waited while I did. "Remember how we talked about setting up phone alerts a ways back? Well I did that for that scumbag football player. And as it turns out, he got into college in Ohio here, for football. And since we were kind of in proximity, I thought we'd pay him a visit, just in case he didn't learn the lesson. Because I think maybe he didn't learn the lesson."

"Kyle? We're here to see Kyle?" I winced at the pitch my voice hit, but couldn't stop myself. "That's your surprise for me?" I was right to be worried.

"You probably should've told her sooner," Hunter said, somehow sounding both laughing and concerned, and Morgan shrugged.

We got to the college campus just as it was about sunrise. I didn't know if there were summer classes, or if there was just always football practice, or what. College was never going to be something Mama and Daddy let me do. The fact that I could maybe try now occurred to me and I sat a minute with that. What would I do? I maybe had the time to think about it.

Hunter drove slowly, easing over speed bumps, and Morgan drummed on the dashboard and looked this way and that. "Allie, roll down your window. We need to use your nose to find him. I don't know what dorm he's in or whatever."

"Use my nose," I said as I obeyed. I didn't think I was ever going to see Kyle Dodd again, much less *smell* Kyle Dodd again. I was already nervous and uncertain about this idea, there was no way Morgan just wanted me to see him and get closure. There was no way Morgan just wanted to talk. I could lie, I thought. I could pretend that I didn't smell him. Maybe he went home after all, for a visit.

But then I did smell him. Leather and body spray and hair gel. He wouldn't be wearing that Varsity jacket, not in summer, not at college, but maybe the leather was his shoes, or a football, or from being in his car.

"Where?" Morgan asked, and I knew I never would've had the chance to lie. Even if she couldn't see my face in the car seat behind her, she could tell that I was stiffened up and pointing like a hunting dog, that my heart was climbed up into my throat and hammering in my ears.

"Just down the way," I said, leaning so that Hunter could see where I was pointing and make the turn. Down a lane of trees that led away from the main cluster of campus buildings, towards dorms maybe, or a lake. I thought I smelled water too. I didn't smell anybody else, though. Kyle was alone as we followed him, as Morgan had Hunter pull over, as she made me get out of the car.

"Wait here," she said, and Hunter slouched in the driver's seat and nodded, pouting a little. She didn't like being left out but she could see the sense in it.

I tried to walk faster than Morgan, to get to Kyle first. Did I have an idea that I wanted him to feel bad for what he did? Yes. But I wasn't going to know if he did, if Morgan got to him first. I didn't have any idea what I was going to say. I didn't have any idea of what to do.

We saw him as the sidewalk led past a piece of woods that had a trail through it, and I had a weird flash of what it might have looked like to him, when he followed me to the woods at the edge of the high school property. What it might have felt like, to come up behind me, intending what he intended. He had headphones on, he didn't hear us. He was jogging, in workout clothes, and he wasn't limping, and I felt Morgan see that and sense her fury increase.

"Kyle!" I yelled, sudden and loud enough for it to cut through, and he stumbled, stopped, pulling his headphones off.

"Allie?" He turned, the whites of his eyes showing, a spike of his fear souring the air. "Allie, what the fuck?" Nobody called me Alleluia, at school. And he was confused, and scared, but also kind of pissed off.

"What do you mean, what the fuck? You attacked me." He made a face like I was stupid, like I was overreacting, and when Morgan strode past me, I didn't try to stop her. He looked from me to her, and then back again and he still somehow didn't get it until she hit him the first time, short and tight and in the diaphragm, so that he folded around her fist and couldn't get in the breath to yell. His headphones clattered onto the ground, still playing one of those stupid country songs that the football boys always liked and blasted before their practice, so that it came up through the woods to the house.

She broke his nose with the next swing and let him take those couple steps back with his hands to his face, wheezing "Hey" before she hit him in the guts again, hit him in the face again, moving fluidly out of the way when he gestured to try and hit her back. She didn't care what he felt. She didn't care if he had anything to say, which I didn't think he did. She was taller, stronger, faster, and she wanted to hurt him. And some small mean part of me let her do it. When he truly faltered, she gathered the front of his shirt in her left hand, so she could hammer in with her right.

I realized almost too late that she wasn't going to stop on her own. "Morgan, no. No, stop it." She hesitated in the swing, hit him again anyway, raised her fist again, and I caught her by the arm and dragged her back a few steps. She didn't let go of his shirt with the other hand, but by the sound of it, his shirt was about ready to let go. "Don't. You don't need to do this. You aren't the one he hurt."

"Aren't I?" she said in such a flash of teeth and anger and bitterness that I let go in surprise and fear. And I had a moment where I thought I could live with that, letting Morgan blame Kyle for everything that happened, instead of Mama. Instead of me. But I couldn't.

I knew what I had to say to her and it just hollowed me out. I took a breath, and steeled myself, and said as clearly and deliberately as I could, "Killing him won't bring Rachel back."

She dropped Kyle immediately and he thudded on the ground like a sack of potatoes. I didn't think he was conscious anymore, but he was alive. I flinched back from her, putting my hands up and ducking my head, but I wasn't fast enough, she punched me in the face and it hurt and shocked me so much that I couldn't even tell where she hit me at first.

But I was a wolf too, and I hit her back. Not with any kind of art, or grace, or even really practice, but I surprised her and probably hurt myself just as much as I hurt her, punching her full in the mouth before she grabbed me by the back of the neck and digging her fingers into my stitches as I squealed, hit me in the stomach once, twice, three times and then dropped me like she'd dropped Kyle and stepped away, pacing in a tight circle, swinging her arms.

I got up slowly, winded, fresh blood trickling hotly down my neck, watching her warily. She didn't go over to Kyle again, she was staring at me. She was giving me the space to choose if I wanted to try to hit her again.

Did I want to try to hit her again? Did I want to fight Morgan? No. No I didn't. Would I, if it hopefully kept all the rest of us alive and also not killing people? Yes.

We stared at each other, breathing hard, and after a moment she shook her head, said, "Fuck it," and spit some blood on the ground before turning to stalk off. I watched her go, heartbroken, relieved. Then I half rolled Kyle over to get at his phone, and it was locked so I pressed buttons until it decided an emergency was happening and dialed 911. I wedged the phone into his hand and ran after Morgan; I had nowhere else to go.

It was full daylight now. Somehow, Hunter had stayed in the vehicle like Morgan told her to, but I could see her face and she was surprised and dismayed when she saw Morgan. She pressed her lips together and looked until she saw me coming along too, and seemed relieved but not any happier.

Morgan got in the car but didn't seem to say anything, though I could see Hunter's lips moving, and then Hunter digging around in her purse until she handed Morgan something. By the time I got in the car, Morgan had what looked like a silky scarf wrapped around her bloody knuckles and was lighting a cigarette. She was like a frayed electric wire, and I didn't know what to expect when I got in the back seat.

Hunter looked at me over her shoulder and sighed a little. "I guess we're going to need to get ice," she said. Morgan didn't say anything, and we drove away before we ever heard a siren.

• • • •

WE WENT THROUGH A DRIVE-thru and ordered breakfasts and coffees and cups of ice and lots of extra napkins. Hunter passed everything around and back and then got on the highway again. At one point she said, "There's a prescription bottle in my purse, and you should give Allie one of them before she gets worse." I started to ask, worse than what, or say I was fine, and that's when I realized that the wheezing noise I thought the air conditioning was making, a weird noise for such a new car, was me. "Maybe you should take one too."

"I'm good," Morgan said, but she turned around in her seat and reached back to drop a little white pill in my hand. I had blood on my hand from me, or from hitting her, but I sat there holding napkins and not doing anything to clean up. "That's an ativan, I think," she said, and Hunter nodded. "You're having a panic attack, probably, and it'll help with that. It's what they'd give you at an ER, probably."

"I got some after you were freaking out so bad in New York," Hunter said, like it was normal to be able to order up the kinds of pills you thought you wanted. I took the pill, drank some more water.

"At least we know the Silvernail knockout drugs are out of your system," Morgan said with a grin, and straighted in her seat again.

"God damn it, Morgan," I said, once I could catch my breath again.

"What? What'd I do?"

"You could've killed him."

"Oh. Yeah, I could've." Like it was no big deal. "Though I guess he wouldn't have learned his lesson then."

"Do you think he did? Learned his lesson?"

"He learned he could still get his ass kicked, and I'll bet he's too embarrassed to try and say who did it. I didn't even break much, I'm sure his football career will remain intact."

"You're so fucking generous," Hunter said, laughing. "Just look at how happy Allie is with her gift."

"Allie doesn't always know what's good for her," Morgan grumbled.

"And you don't get to decide that for me!" I didn't know I was going to yell, but I sure did. "How was this good for me? What did it help?"

"It was an asskicking he deserved and that you only kind of gave him in the first place. What's done is done and you don't ever need to think about it again, I won't bring it up again, scout's honor."

"You...do you think that doing this cleaned the slate? That beating him up like that *exorcized* what he did?"

"Just let me know if it worked, okay?" I heard the grin in her voice and I wanted to punch her. Punch her seat. Yell again. I didn't do any of those things, maybe because the pill worked or maybe because I saw her doing those things and there was only so much like Morgan I wanted to be. Needed to be.

I looked out the window, thought about every time I'd been in a car just looking out the window and waiting to go where people took me. Even now, after everything that happened, I was just a passenger. But I'd decided it, I'd decided to go with the Culvers, go with the family my blood called to, even when I was driving a stolen car with a wolf in the back. I'd made that choice over and over. It felt like my only choice, but it felt like the right choice too. Until this last time, and I still got back in the car.

I held ice to my face and wiped blood off my neck or maybe just smeared it around on my skin. I drank some more water and I didn't know how long we'd been driving when I finally asked "Where are we going?"

Morgan was quiet long enough that I thought she wouldn't answer. She hadn't turned on the radio. "Home," she finally said.

We went home.

We drove to the clearing in the pines where we used to park the cars, right now just Hunter's Range Rover, breaking pine boughs as we pulled through, so the resinous scent rose around us in the warm summer air. We got out and stretched, shuffling our boots in the sandy soil, listening to the birds. We walked past the still, shrouded and cold in its pine boughs. We walked past the chickens who scolded us for coming near, who scolded us for leaving them, and there were chickens there who had never seen people, who had hatched while we were gone, and never knew that we would come back, because who knew what kind of a memory a chicken has anyway. We walked through the pines until we started to smell the smoke, the burned wood from when the aunts were first taken and this whole mess started.

Sela should be here, I thought, but she was with Sidney and they were both safe. Fran. Mama should be here, but she wasn't a wolf, and she was the reason all of this happened. Dulcie should be here. Rachel.

Morgan didn't stop, though, didn't hesitate. She picked her way through the ruin, until she was standing at the pile of stones that had been the big fireplace.

"When me and Fran were little, I took a screwdriver and stood in the fireplace one summer, put my name on one of the big rocks up inside," she said. "Rachel gave me a spanking for tracking ashes all over the place, I think it was maybe the last time she did that, for all the good it ever did. She might've given Fran a spanking too, for not stopping me. I don't remember. But I had to scrub the floors and beat out the rugs and all that, but I don't think she ever really realized why I was in there to begin with. Oh yeah, I had to clean out the fireplace too, until she could white glove it. That took a long time. And she had to buy the gloves." I laughed a little and sobbed at the same time, and it hurt to do it. It hurt to think about it, because I could picture it so clearly, and she was gone.

Morgan bent, and the rocks clacked around, and when she turned around, her knuckles were bleeding again, and she was holding a big flat rock that had been up in the fireplace for years and years. And it had MORGAN etched into it, the letters a little bit lopsided.

"I don't know why I never told her. Probably because it wouldn't've gotten me out of all that cleaning. Fran didn't know I did it either, Fran was being the good daughter and ministering to the sick or spinning straw into gold or something. And I don't know what Rachel would've said if she'd known."

"Daughter mine..." I said, even though that hurt too, but something caught my eye, and I waded into the stones as well. I picked one up that said RACHEL on it. Hunter gave a quiet little gasp of surprise.

"Fuck," Morgan said and we all laughed.

"You didn't tell her because it's okay to have something that's just yours," I said.

"I guess."

Without really saying anything, without really planning anything, we picked around a little more. The family's genera-tional cast iron still seemed like it might be usable. It all needed to be cleaned and reseasoned, but none of it cracked apart from the fire, somehow. There was still a foundation here, though I didn't know anything about construction, if it was sound or not. Rachel and I had just reshingled the damn roof, I thought ruefully.

I'd just gotten a splinter and was working it out of my finger when I thought I heard the jingle of a dog's tags and raised my head, confused.

Morgan snapped around entirely, but she was caught off balance when Dio charged out of the pines and took her out at the knees, then danced and wriggled and whined around her, licking her face furiously as she tried to grab him up and pet him and hug him.

"How did—" I started to say, but Hunter was smiling, and Morgan finally pulled Dio into her lap and just hugged him against her, her face pressed into his neck, and Luke and Joe also came out of the trees.

"I really hoped he'd know the way," Luke said.

"What the fuck?" Morgan asked, but she wasn't angry for once. Dio was still wriggling so much I couldn't really see her face, but if it was me, and if that was my dog, I knew I'd be bawling.

"Hello," Joe said, kind of waving, and it struck me as just so funny, or my emotions were all tangled up, that I started laughing, and then I went to hug him. He was surprised, but after a second hugged me back. When we parted, we were both blushing, and Morgan had gotten to her feet, Dio still pressing himself against her legs, wagging so hard he was knocking himself around, and so knocking her around.

"Dio, you're gonna knock me over again," she said, putting her hand on his head. "Luke, what the fuck."

"If you didn't want us to find you, you would've taken the tracker off," Luke said calmly, patiently, and I looked at Morgan. I would've thought she'd have taken the tracker off the second Silvernail grabbed me instead of her.

She shrugged. "What can I say, I'm complicated."

"And sentimental, and what else has she said?" He looked at me, and I shrugged too.

"Morgan says a lot of things," I said, and Hunter laughed.

"Doesn't she though!"

"But I figured you'd want your dog," Luke said, glancing around a little. It looked like the hand pump might have gone untouched by the fire, we would have to see. "Fran mentioned him, so we went and got him from Sela. It took a lot of hot dogs to convince him that he didn't want to eat my face, actually."

"That's my boy," Morgan said, grinning. "Right Dio? You love eating faces." Dio dog-grinned up at her.

"So, now that we're here, you got any idea how to build a house?" I asked Morgan.

"Nope," she said. "But you saved those Foxfire books right? Isn't there a house building tutorial in there?"

"There's a log cabin, yeah."

"There, perfect. We'll figure it out."

"We could stay around and help," Joe said, shyly but firmly, not looking at Luke. "Luke's done construction."

"Yeah sure, just volunteer us," Luke said, actually laughing for once. "Yeah, we'll help, if you'll have us."

"Luke I never took you for a homemaker," Morgan said with a sly grin and Hunter cackled.

"You're so fucking funny," Luke said. I think we were all a little goofy, relieved. It was a good combination of things, a way to balance out the grief and the anger. Exhaustion.

"We're going to have to go and get all the rest of the dogs," I said to Morgan. "Sela and Sidney aren't going to want to take care of them themselves." Sela and Sidney might want to come too, I thought.

"And that's a joy, let me tell you. You haven't lived until you've driven a car with like, ten dogs in it."

"Or we could drive two cars with five dogs each?" Like when Rachel and I came and got them, I almost said, but didn't. That knot was in my throat again.

Morgan rolled her eyes, then shook her head. "No no, that just lessens the experience, come on Allie. We want authentic pineyisms here."

I forced a smile. "You told me that isn't a real thing."

"Well yeah, no, it isn't a real thing."

"God damn it Morgan."

"Allie, language. I'm shocked."

"It's because you've been such a bad influence," I said, and I reached down to pet Dio as well. He was the dog I'd spent the most time with, when I came here, and he swiped my hand with his tongue but he had eyes only for Morgan.

"We had catching up to do, I'm sure you'll even out now that the cram session is over."

"*Is* it over?" I asked, and I meant more than the cram session. More than werewolf catch up. I meant too much, and just couldn't say any of it. We all stood there in silence for a few minutes, just the pine sounds around us, and the chickens, and Dio panting.

"It is for now," Morgan said finally, like a sigh. The fury she was feeling, the hurt, it all just sat beneath the surface like a pot about to boil over, but she had a lid on it, and I had a lid on mine, and that was about all any of us could ask for right now. Not a single one of us knew the right way to feel, other than relief, and even that hurt.

But for now, we were alive. We were safe. And we were home.

## Acknowledgements

I know I already thanked you, the reader, in my author notes, and I have a few additional (evergreen really) thanks

Thank you to Jim for your love and support.

Thank you to Premee! You know what you did.

Thank you to Lennon, for proofreading, and putting up with this circus.

Thank you to my Eternal Gratitude patrons I appreciate that you believe in me, and your commitment to my writing! (Heather, Sheryl, and Brian [look, this is the one The Brians are mentioned in!])

And thanks to all my new readers, who heard that these weren't like other werewolves, and have now come on this road trip with me!

## About the Author

Jennifer R. Donohue grew up at the Jersey Shore and now lives in central New York with her husband and their Dobermans. She works at her local public library where she also facilitates a writing workshop. Her work has appeared in *Apex Magazine*, *Escape Pod*, *Fantasy*, *The Deadlands*, *Fusion Fragment*, and elsewhere. Her debut novel, Exit Ghost, is available now. She posts @AuthorizedMusings.bsky.social and you can subscribe to her Patreon for a new short story every month:https://www.patreon.com/JenniferRDonohue

**Further work by Jennifer R. Donohue**

*Exit Ghost*

*The Drowned Heir*

*Between the Blood and the Sun*

***The Learn to Howl Trilogy***

*Learn to Howl*

*Baying the Moon*

*The Company of Wolves*

***Other books in the Run With the Hunted series***

Run With the Hunted

Run With the Hunted 2: Ctrl Alt Delete

Run With the Hunted 3: Standard Operating Procedure

Run With the Hunted 4: VIP

Run With the Hunted 5: Insert Coin to Play

Run With the Hunted 6: Burned Asset

Run With the Hunted 7: The Casino Job